Edited by Douglas Glover

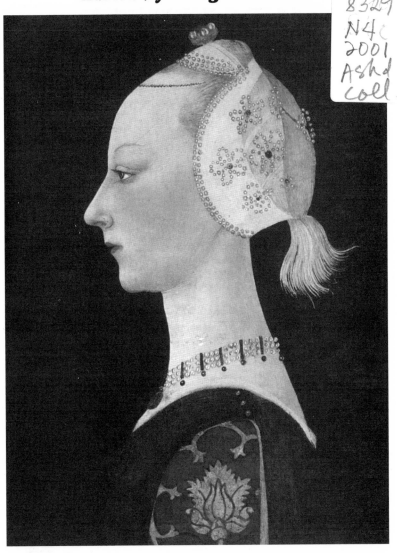

Best Canadian Stories
01

We acknowledge the support of the Canada Council for the Arts, the Ontario Arts Council and the Government of Canada through the Book Publishing Industry Development Program for our publishing activities.

"Floating Bridge" by Alice Munro was first published in *The New Yorker*. "Standing on Richards" by George Bowering first appeared in *Malahat Review*. "Religious Knowledge" by Cynthia Flood was originally published in *Prism International*. "The Alcoholist" by Bill Gaston originally appeared in *Event*. "the first motion of love" by Kevin Armstrong was first published in *Grain*.

The following magazines were consulted: *Algonquin Roundtable Review, Antigonish Review, Blood & Aphorisms, Canadian Fiction Magazine, The Canadian Forum, The Capilano Review, Descant, Event, The Fiddlehead, Geist, Grain, Malahat Review, The New Quarterly, The New Yorker, Paragraph, Prism International, Prairie Fire, Quarry, Saturday Night* and *Windsor Review*.

ISBN 0 7780 1187 9 (hardcover)
ISBN 0 7780 1188 7 (softcover)
ISSN 0703 9476

Cover art: Master of the Castello Nativity
Book design by Michael Macklem

ONTARIO ARTS COUNCIL
CONSEIL DES ARTS DE L'ONTARIO

Printed in Canada

PUBLISHED IN CANADA BY OBERON PRESS

LEON ROOKE
THE YELLOW HOUSE 9

ALICE MUNRO
FLOATING BRIDGE 15

RAMONA DEARING
AN APOLOGY 44

GEORGE BOWERING
STANDING ON RICHARDS 62

CYNTHIA FLOOD
RELIGIOUS KNOWLEDGE 79

BILL GASTON
THE ALCOHOLIST 101

KEVIN ARMSTRONG
THE FIRST MOTION OF LOVE 113

CHARLOTTE GILL
THE ART OF MEDICINE 125

Contributions for the thirty-second volume, published or unpublished, should be sent to Oberon Press, 400–350 Sparks Street, Ottawa, Ontario KIR 7S8 before 31 March, 2002. All manuscripts should enclose a stamped self-addressed envelope.

INTRODUCTION

I love the whimsical purity of Leon Rooke's stories, the way verisimilitude goes out the window, whole mythic universes appear in a dozen sentences, plots deploy around characters that are nothing more than voice and desire, and magic happens. In "The Yellow House," two families—one moribund and fearful, the other vibrant and healthy—live side-by-side in some fictional other-world. One day a boy from the healthy house kisses the sultry sister from the sickly house, and suddenly fish fly in the air, health blossoms, love floods the story like a "blinding yellow light."

Amazingly, the same kiss appears in Alice Munro's "Floating Bridge," the tale of a young woman undergoing chemotherapy while her social-worker husband barely conceals his crush on a girl he's supposed to be helping. Jinny meets a teenage boy who drives her into the night on a dark, strange road through a bog. Walking out onto a floating bridge that rises and falls with their footsteps, they kiss, and suddenly: "Jinny felt a rain of compassion, almost like laughter. A swish of tender hilarity, getting the better of her sores and hollows, for the time given."

A more sinister kiss turns up in Ramona Dearing's "An Apology," which tells the story of a bent priest on trial for mistreating boys in a Newfoundland orphanage. "'You kissed the boy?' 'Yes, many times. Like a mother.' 'On the lips?' 'Yes, sir. Like a mother would.'" Dearing does a fine job of making her priest a credible, vulnerable character as his carapace of denial and self-pity gradually slips away.

And George Bowering's flamboyantly eccentric "Standing on Richards"—the story of a retired professor who decides to become a prostitute of the mind in Vancouver's Red Light district, selling his brain though not his body—ends with a kiss. After winning an argument with a trick (the only one who picks him up), a hair-splitting scholarly debate on whether he is selling his mind or his brain and which is worth more, Bowering's hero smiles. "'How about a kiss?' he said. What the hell. I gave him a kiss."

In Cynthia Flood's "Religious Knowledge" a girl reacts hysterically to sexual hijinks at her boarding-school. Her behaviour inspires impatience and anger amongst her friends and school officials, till a spinster teacher finally pieces together the story of childhood molestation by the girl's Anglican priest father: "...in her ears sound the only lines that have stayed with her from *Murder {in the Cathedral}*: 'the torn girl trembling by the mill-stream....'"

This year Bill Gaston contributes "The Alcoholist," a story I admire for its mellifluous flights of language as well as for its outré subject matter: a man whose pathologically developed sense of smell and taste have led him to a career —as an alcoholic drink-taster and consultant—and ultimately to his death. "Addiction was an equation too. In truth, a marriage. And disease its necessary divorce."

Kevin Armstrong's "the first motion of love" is the sly tale of a naïve young Canadian who finds and loses love in a New Zealand brothel while simultaneously and hilariously discovering his identity in the works of the New Zealand novelist C. K. Stead, to whom the story is addressed as a letter. "How perfect. No, how perfectly *Canadian*."

And finally there is Charlotte Gill's "The Art of Medicine," the story of a medical student who has an affair with her instructor, grows depressed and flunks her courses, and the parallel misadventures of her maladroit roommate Colette, an unkempt, weepy grad-student-cum-witch who has an affair with a man in her assertiveness-training seminar and finds herself pregnant. "She spread her arms wide and pointed down at herself. What kind of a mother would I make? You knew exactly the kind of mother she'd make."

DOUGLAS GLOVER

The Yellow House

Leon Rooke

In our family we were always sick, we were always dying from one thing or another, death's face occupied every wall and window, no-one ever went anywhere for fear of giving up the ghost in a strange place.

Which to our mind every other place was. Strange. And strangest of all, the pretty yellow house across the lane where men and women of incomprehensible gaiety, children by the score, were ever arriving: picnics on the lawn by the seashore, platter upon platter of dazzling foods, calisthenics, cartwheels, bocce games and the like. The air charged with laughter, mirthful shouts, the barking of dogs, all as vigorous women pushed prams up and down-hill, gave chase to errant balls, the odd, runaway baby. Then, spent, adults and children alike all stripped down to the bare vestiges of decency, taking the sun on the green grass until the day's last rays were no more.

By night, their songs wafting our way. A kingdom of happiness the yellow house was.

Not so, ours. Waylaid by a thousand maladies, for one of us simply to stand up and slowly cross a room was a torture, the floor groaning just as we were ourselves groaning, although of course we did from time to time make these crossings, not even in an infirmary such as ours could one remain in bed forever. Each of us muttering to ourselves, We will never get better, the end is coming.

Dear parents, should I perish before nightfall please see that all my worldly goods pass on to my sister, Precilla, as for instance my little fire-engine wagon with the red wheels, my Sakimoto red-lipped doll, these worn slippers, this tatty red nightgown which really should be washed before you even consider throwing it about your shoulders.

We were always getting worse, never better. During the rare occurrence when someone did no-one had a pleasant word to say. We knew such improvement would not last long. A day or two, the odd enchanted hour, then the party would be dropping back into bed, depleted beyond all human reckoning, as we all were, beyond human reckoning. We were shut away, window and door were ever closed, our needs were few, food was scarcely an issue, since to have an appetite, to have desire of any kind, was all but inconceivable. We were awash in hopelessness as one would be in a dingy on the stormy sea, God had deserted us, the world had deserted us, it had always been this way, our condition ever the same, we were born to it, all of us were, grandmother and grandfather, parents, the Geeks, who one day just happened to arrive. We heard scuffling feet, laboriously we rolled over, opened our eyes and there the Geeks were, all seven of them, of an age roughly corresponding to our own, a family likely smitten with the syndrome that carried our name, each too weak to advance another step, certainly too weak to offer explanation, and which of us would have had strength to listen, as for that, speech generally was out of the question for our lot. Nothing but groans, cries of woe, yelps of pain, tears, these could hardly be called speech, and it was this way, it had been this way for as long as any of us could remember, certainly long before the arrival of those Geeks, who, it should be said, were worse off than we were, if such is possible, this in large part because of the smell each individually conveyed, collectively, more so, a sour brinish odour, ether and egg-rot, that putrid medicinal tinge that one always associates with death, this baked into them. But then again I suppose we all transported this sickly odour, certainly our parents and grandparents did. The odour had soaked into the walls and flooring, into the carpets and lampshades, everywhere, which was the explanation for why at least one window had to be kept open always, even in cruellest winter. That one open window explaining, too, why those in our house were so acutely aware of the incessant activities at the yellow house across the lane, a picture of perfection perched upon green hills rolling up from the seashore.

Our interest was aroused, it could be said that not much went on over there of which we long remained in ignorance, the train of prams pushed uphill and downhill by vigorous women, generations in transition, now the pram children grown up and themselves pushing bigger and brighter prams, though still, through all of those years, the bocce games, the headstands, the picnics, the beautiful foods, such beautiful people, why them and not us. Horrific, I will have you know, as in the meantime Grandfather died, Grandmother did, the parents, God help them, six Geeks dead, puppets, you might say, disengaged from their strings or a rank of dominoes toppled over, never those three of us remaining now to know who those dead Geeks were or by what circumstance they entered our gate rather than another.

Eons back, in the dark ravages of time—I should have told you this at the start, pray, forgive me—our ancestors established a cemetery off there at the dome of the hill, such a pretty resting place, but over the centuries the leaning stones gradually crept downhill, fanning off to sit among the arcade of coconut palms on one side, the lagoon waters on the other. Advancing our way through a savanna of tall grasses that hid away a barn or two, sheds specific to ancient days when at least some of us must have eked out a small living, satisfied somehow freehold arrangements peculiar to the time and place, in any event these graves now shock up against the backside of our very dwelling. This sprawling cemetery a city unto itself, it might be said, though said in error, since so much of ourselves repose there.

Such a panorama this cemetery is, with green hills rising in the distance, coconut palms, banana trees, and behind them cloud-becloaked mountains in which thread numerous rivers which in the rainy season feed the long fingers of the lagoon, and not far as seen through our open window, one untidy peach tree in warfare with the tall grasses, pampas and the like, no less than with the tumbledown stakes, the lattice-work, once erected in support of that lone peach tree.

Our parents, while alive, intermittently spoke of the glories of those peaches, a glory confined to their youth, alas, since none in mine and my sister's lifetime were endowed with the fortitude to hike down there and claim the luscious fruit.

How could we, we who could barely breathe, a people who could barely lift the dipper to the mouth when riddled by fever or draw up the covers when shamed by cold, so, yes, I say, in the interim so many of our numbers gone, there remaining in our sad family at the present moment one Geek more or less of my age, sexless, as I suppose I must be, despairing, as I know I was, the both of us sharing but the flutter of random breath, on our hot backsides here, our graves open and waiting, our end at hand. And the third survivor, my young sister Precilla, hardly any better, you would have thought, with no place to turn, you would think.

Thus, then, to imagine the surprise, the wonder the Geek child and I experienced as, this morning, coming awake to the sight of Precilla at the open window, we heard her say—"There is a young man from the yellow house down there picking our peaches. He is smiling at me. Unless I am sadly mistaken in a moment he will arrive here with his peaches. He will ask for my hand in marriage. For love's sake I believe I shall say yes. Nowhere has it been written that you and I, dear brother, and you, dear Geek, should forever suffer, as this family has suffered. God help me, I almost feel well. I almost feel happiness. I feel faint with wonder. He is such a vision."

How could this be?

Precilla with her face lit by sunshine, a hint of colour in her cheeks, at her throat a glitter of stones, her hair tied by blue string into two high bundles above each ear like miniature stands of wheat, on her thin frame a sleeveless summer dress, bedaubed with gay colours, a party dress, it might almost be called.

Where had she got such a dress?

"Here he comes," she said. "I can see his lips forming the words."

I lifted myself up. A cool breeze had come up. Sunlight lit the window, casting my sister's face into an all but unrecognizable radiance. As for that, the Geek girl, if girl she was, wore on her face a look of strange exaltation, of triumph, such as I had never seen before. This emanating from a girl whom I—bound by sorrow, by self-pity—had scarcely ever troubled myself to study before. She possessed a sultriness that I found intoxicating. Through what magic, I wondered, had these two suddenly become so beautiful?

And there the young man was, at the window, he could have been my age. In another world I could have been that young man at a window, let's say at a window of the yellow house, my lips forming those same words this young man's lips were forming. A hand of Precilla's was at rest on the window-ledge. The young man raised her hand to his lips.

They remained there, lips pressing her fingers, their eyes closed.

Out at sea storm clouds were forming, tumbling and turning. A tumult of wind swept low over the water. Over the roof of the yellow house could be seen schools of silver fish in flight inches above the water. School upon school of these silver fish, all flying.

And here was coming to my own bed the surviving Geek, coming with scarcely a groan, the very picture of blossoming health.

The wind swept through these fish, and now came a fierce darkening, and hard rain, and falling from the sky thousands upon thousands of these shining fish, the Geek person sliding between my sheets, my sister and her young man kissing in the window, and in the next second our entire sick bay under a flood of blinding yellow light.

Floating Bridge

Alice Munro

One time, she had left him. The immediate reason was fairly trivial. He had joined a couple of the Young Offenders ("Yo-yos" was what he called them) in gobbling up a gingerbread cake she had just made, and had been intending to serve after a meeting that evening. Unobserved—at least by Neal and the Yo-yos—she had left the house and gone to sit in a three-sided shelter on the main street, where the city bus stopped twice a day. She had never been in there before, and she had a couple of hours to wait. She sat and read everything that had been written on or cut into those wooden walls. Various initials loved each other 4 ever. Laurie G. sucked cock. Dunk Cultis was a fag. So was Mr. Garner (Math).

Eat Shit. H. W. Gange rules. God hates filth. Kevin S. Is Dead meat. Amanda W is beautiful and sweet and I wish they did not put her in jail because I miss her with all my heart. I want to fuck V.P. Ladies have to sit here and read this disgusting dirty things what you write. Fuck them.

Looking at this barrage of human messages—and puzzling in particular over the heartfelt, very neatly written sentence concerning Amanda W—Jinny wondered if people were alone when they wrote such things. And she went on to imagine herself sitting here or in some similar place, waiting for a bus, alone as she would surely be if she went ahead with the plan she was set on now. Would she be compelled to make statements on public walls?

She felt herself connected at present to those people who had had to write certain things down—connected by her feelings of anger and petty outrage (perhaps it was petty?), and by her excitement at what she was doing to Neal, to pay him back. It occurred to her that the life she was carrying herself into might not give her anybody to be effectively angry at, or anybody who owed her anything, who could possibly be rewarded or punished or truly affected by what she might do. She was not, after all, somebody people flocked to. And yet she was choosy, in her own way.

The bus was still not in sight when she got up and walked home. Neal was not there. He was returning the boys to the school, and by the time he got back, somebody had already arrived for the meeting. She told Neal what she'd done, but only when she was well over it and it could be turned into a joke. In fact, it became a joke she told in company—leaving out or just describing in a general way the things she'd read on the walls.

"Would you ever have thought to come after me?" she said to Neal.

"Of course. Given time."

The oncologist had a priestly demeanour and even wore a black turtleneck shirt under a white smock—an outfit that suggested he had just come from some ceremonial mixing and dosing. His skin was young and smooth—it looked like butterscotch. On the dome of his head, there was just a faint black growth of hair, a delicate sprouting, very like the fuzz Jinny was sporting herself, though hers was brown-

16

ish-grey, like mouse fur. At first, Jinny had wondered if he could possibly be a patient as well as a doctor. Then, whether he had adopted this style to make the patients more comfortable. More likely it was a transplant. Or just the way he liked to wear his hair.

You couldn't ask him. He came from Syria or Jordan—someplace where doctors kept their dignity. His courtesies were frigid.

"Now," he said, "I do not wish to give a wrong impression."

She went out of the air-conditioned building into the stunning glare of a late afternoon, in August, in Ontario. Sometimes the sun burned through, sometimes it stayed behind thin clouds—it was just as hot either way. She saw the car detach itself from its place at the curb and make its way down the street to pick her up. It was a light-blue, shimmery, sickening colour. Lighter blue where the rust spots had been painted over. Its stickers said, "I Know I Drive a Wreck But You Should See My House," and "Honour Thy Mother—Earth," and (this was more recent) "Use Pesticide—Kill Weeds, Promote Cancer."

Neal came around to help her.

"She's in the car," he said. There was an eager note in his voice which registered vaguely as a warning or a plea. A buzz around him, a tension, that told Jinny it wasn't time to give him her news, if "news" was what you'd call it. When Neal was around other people, even one person other than Jinny, his behaviour changed, becoming more animated, enthusiastic, ingratiating. Jinny was not bothered by that anymore—they had been together for 21 years. And she herself changed—as a reaction, she used to think—becoming more reserved and slightly ironic. Some masquerades were necessary, or just too habitual to be dropped.

Like Neal's antique appearance—the bandanna headband, the rough grey ponytail, the little gold earring that caught the light like the gold rims around his teeth, and his shaggy outlaw clothes.

While Jinny had been seeing the doctor, Neal had been picking up the girl who was going to help them with their life now. He knew her from the Correctional Institute for Young Offenders, where he was a teacher and she had worked in the kitchen. The Correctional Institute was just outside the town where they lived, about 30 miles away. The girl had quit her kitchen job a few months ago and taken a job looking after a farm household where the mother was sick. Luckily she was now free.

"What happened to the woman?" Jinny had said. "Did she die?"

Neal said, "She went into the hospital."

"Same deal."

Neal had spent nearly all his spare time, in the years Jinny had been with him, organizing and carrying out campaigns. Not just political campaigns (those, too) but efforts to preserve historic buildings and bridges and cemeteries, to keep trees from being cut down both along the town streets and in isolated patches of old forest, to save rivers from poisonous runoff and choice land from developers and the local population from casinos. Letters and petitions were always being written, government departments lobbied, posters distributed, protests organized. The front room of their house had been the scene of rages of indignation (which gave people a lot of satisfaction, Jinny thought) and of confused propositions and arguments, and Neal's nervy buoyancy. Now it was suddenly emptied. The front room would become the sickroom. It made her think of when she first walked into the house, straight from her parents' split-level with the swag curtains, and imagined all those shelves filled with books, wooden shutters on the windows, and those beautiful Middle Eastern rugs she always forgot the name of, on the varnished floor. On the one bare wall, the Canaletto print she had bought for her room at college— *Lord Mayor's Day on the Thames*. She had actually put that up, though she never noticed it anymore.

They rented a hospital bed—they didn't really need it yet, but it was better to get one while you could, because they were often in short supply. Neal thought of everything. He hung up some heavy curtains that were discards from a friend's family room. Jinny thought them very ugly, but she knew now that there comes a time when ugly and beautiful serve pretty much the same purpose, when anything you look at is just a peg to hang the unruly sensations of your body on.

Jinny was 42, and until recently she had looked younger than her age. Neal was sixteen years older than she was. So she had thought that in the natural course of things she would be in the position he was in now, and she had sometimes worried about how she would manage it. Once, when she was holding his hand in bed before they went to sleep, his warm and present hand, she had thought that she would hold or touch this hand, at least once, when he was dead. And no matter how long she had foreseen this, she would not be able to credit it. To think of his not having some knowledge of this moment and of her brought on a kind of emotional vertigo, the sense of a horrid drop.

And yet—an excitement. The unspeakable excitement you feel when a galloping disaster promises to release you from all responsibility for your own life. Then from shame you must compose yourself, and stay very quiet.

"Where are you going?" he had said, when she withdrew her hand.

"No place. Just turning over."

She didn't know if Neal had any such feeling, now that it had turned out to be her. She had asked him if he was used to the idea yet. He shook his head.

She said, "Me neither."

Then she said, "Just don't let the Grief Counsellors in. They could be hanging around already. Wanting to make a pre-emptive strike."

"Don't harrow me," he said, in a voice of rare anger.

"Sorry."

"You don't always have to take the lighter view."

"I know," she said. But the fact was that, with so much going on and present events grabbing so much other attention, she found it hard to take any view at all.

"This is Helen," Neal said. "This is who is going to look after us from now on. She won't stand for any nonsense, either."

"Good for her," said Jinny. She put out her hand, once she was settled in the car. But the girl might not have seen it, low down between the two front seats.

Or she might not have known what to do. Neal had said that she came from an unbelievable situation, an absolutely barbaric family. Things had gone on that you could not imagine going on in this day and age. An isolated farm, a widower—a tyrannical, deranged, incestuous old man— with a mentally deficient daughter and the two girl children. Helen, the older one, who had run away at the age of fourteen after beating up on the old man, had been sheltered by a neighbour, who phoned the police. And then the police had come and got the younger sister and made both children wards of the Children's Aid. The old man and his daughter—that is, the childrens' father and their mother—were both placed in a psychiatric hospital. Foster parents took Helen and her sister, who were mentally and physically normal. They were sent to school and had a miserable time there, having to start first grade in their teens. But they both learned enough to be employable.

When Neal had started the car up, the girl decided to speak.

"You picked a hot enough day to be out in," she said. It was the sort of thing she might have heard people say, to start a conversation. She spoke in a hard, flat tone of antagonism and distrust, but even that, Jinny knew by now, should not be taken personally. It was just the way some people sounded—particularly country people—in this part of the world.

"If you're hot, you can turn the air-conditioner on," Neal said. "We've got the old-fashioned kind—just roll down all the windows."

The turn they made at the next corner was one Jinny had not expected. "We have to go to the hospital," Neal said. "Helen's sister works there, and she's got something Helen wants to pick up. Isn't that right, Helen?"

Helen said, "Yeah. My good shoes."

"Helen's good shoes." Neal looked up at the mirror. "Miss Helen Rosie's good shoes."

"My name's not Helen Rosie," said Helen. It seemed as if it was not the first time she had said this.

"I just call you that because you have such a rosy face," Neal said.

"I have not."

"You do. Doesn't she, Jinny? Jinny agrees with me—you've got a rosy face. Miss Helen Rosie-Face."

The girl did have tender pink skin. Jinny had also noticed her nearly white lashes and eyebrows, her blond baby-wool hair, and her mouth, which had an oddly naked look, not just the normal look of a mouth without lipstick. A fresh-out-of-the-egg look was what she had, as if one layer of skin were still missing, one final growth of coarser, grownup hair. She must be susceptible to rashes and infections, quick to show scrapes and bruises, to get sores around the mouth and sties between her white lashes, Jinny thought. Yet she didn't look frail. Her shoulders were broad, she was lean but big-boned. She didn't look stupid, either, though she had a head-on expression like a calf's or a deer's. Everything must be right on the surface with her, her attention and the whole of her personality coming straight at you, with an innocent and—to Jinny—a disagreeable power.

They drove up to the main doors of the hospital, then, following Helen's directions, swung around to the back. People in hospital dressing-gowns, some trailing their IVs, had come outside to smoke.

"Helen's sister works in the laundry," Neal said. "What's her name, Helen? What's your sister's name?"

"Muriel," said Helen. "Stop here. Okay. Here."

They were in a parking-lot at the back of a wing of the hospital. There were no doors on the ground floor except a loading door, shut tight. Helen was getting out of the car.

"You know how to find your way in?" Neal said.

"Easy."

The fire escape stopped four or five feet above the ground, but she was able to grab hold of the railing and swing herself up, maybe wedging a foot against a loose brick, in a matter of seconds. Neal was laughing.

"Go get 'em, girl!" he said.

"Isn't there any other way?" said Jinny.

Helen had run up to the third floor and disappeared.

"If there is, she ain't a-gonna use it," Neal said.

"Full of gumption," said Jinny, with an effort.

"Otherwise she'd never have broken out," he said. "She needed all the gumption she could get."

Jinny was wearing a wide-brimmed straw hat. She took it off and began to fan herself.

Neal said, "Sorry. There doesn't seem to be any shade to park in."

"Do I look too startling?" Jinny said. He was used to her asking that.

"You're fine. There's nobody around here anyway."

"The doctor I saw today wasn't the same one I'd seen before. I think this one was more important. The funny thing was he had a scalp that looked about like mine. Maybe he does it to put the patients at ease."

She meant to go on and tell him what the doctor had said, but the fanning took up most of her energy. He watched the building.

"I hope to Christ they didn't haul her up for getting in the wrong way," he said. "She is just not a gal for whom the rules were made."

After several minutes, he let out a whistle.

"Here she comes now. Here-she-comes. Headin' down the homestretch. Will she, will she, will she have enough sense to stop before she jumps? Look before she leaps? Will she, will she—nope. Nope. Unh-*unh*."

Helen had no shoes in her hands. She got into the car and banged the door shut and said, "Stupid idiots. First I get up there and this asshole gets in my way. Where's your tag? You gotta have a tag. I seen you come in off the fire escape, you can't do that. Okay, okay, I gotta see my sister. You

23

can't see her now, she's not on her break. I know that. That's why I come in off the fire escape. I just need to pick something up. I don't want to talk to her. I'm not goin' to take up her time. I just gotta pick something up. Well, you can't. Well, I can. Well, you can't. And then I start to holler *Muriel, Muriel.* All their machines goin'. It's two hundred degrees in there. I don't know where she is, can she hear me or not. But she comes tearing out and as soon as she sees me—Oh, shit. Oh, shit, she says, I went and forgot. She forgot. I phoned her up last night and reminded her, but there she is. Shit, she forgot. I could've beat her up. Now you get out, he says. Go downstairs and out. Not by the fire escape, because it's illegal. Piss on him."

Neal was laughing and laughing and shaking his head.

Jinny said, "Could we just start driving now and get some air? I don't think fanning is doing a lot of good."

"Fine," said Neal, and started the car and backed and turned around, and once more they were passing the familiar front of the hospital, with the same or different smokers parading by in their dreary hospital clothes with their IVs. "Helen will just have to tell us where to go."

He called into the back seat, "Helen."

"What?"

"Which way do we turn now to get to where your sister lives? Where your shoes are."

"We're not goin' to their place, so I'm not telling you. You done me one favour and that's enough." Helen sat as far forward as she could, pushing her head between Neal's seat and Jinny's.

They slowed down, turned into a side street. "That's silly," Neal said. "You're going 30 miles away, and you might not get back here for a while. You might need those shoes." No answer. He tried again. "Or don't you know the way? Don't you know the way from here?"

"I know it, but I'm not telling."

"So we're just going to have to drive around and around till you get ready to tell us."

They were driving through a part of town that Jinny had not seen before. They drove very slowly and made frequent turns, so that hardly any breeze went through the car. A boarded-up factory, discount stores, pawnshops. "Cash, Cash, Cash," said a flashing sign above barred windows. But there were houses, disreputable-looking old duplexes, and the sort of single wooden houses that were put up quickly, during the Second World War. In front of a corner store, some children were sucking on Popsicles.

Helen spoke to Neal. "You're just wasting your gas."

"North of town?" Neal said. "South of town? North, south, east, west, Helen, tell us which is best." On Neal's face there was an expression of conscious, helpless silliness. His whole being was invaded. He was brimming with foolish bliss.

"You're just stubborn," Helen said.

"You'll see how stubborn."

"I am, too. I'm just as stubborn as what you are."

It seemed to Jinny that she could feel the blaze of Helen's cheek, which was so close to hers. And she could certainly hear the girl's breathing, hoarse and thick with excitement and showing some trace of asthma.

The sun had burned through the clouds again. It was still high and brassy in the sky. Neal swung the car onto a street lined with heavy old trees, and somewhat more respectable houses.

"Better here?" he said to Jinny. "More shade for you?" He spoke in a lowered, confidential tone, as if what was going on in the car could be set aside for a moment. It was all nonsense.

"Taking the scenic route," he said, pitching his voice again toward the back seat. "Taking the scenic route today, courtesy of Miss Helen Rosie-Face."

"Maybe we ought to just go on," Jinny said. "Maybe we ought to just go on home."

Helen broke in, almost shouting. "I don't want to stop nobody from getting home."

"Then you can just give me some directions," Neal said. He was trying hard to get his voice under control, to get some ordinary sobriety into it. And to banish the smile, which kept slipping back in place no matter how often he swallowed it.

Half a slow block more, and Helen groaned. "If I got to, I guess I got to," she said.

It was not very far that they had to go. They passed a subdivision, and Neal, speaking again to Jinny, said, "No creek that I can see. No estates either."

Jinny said, "What?"

"Amber Creek Estates. On the sign. They don't care what they say anymore. Nobody even expects them to explain it."

"Turn," said Helen.

"Left or right?"

"At the wrecker's."

They went past a wrecking yard, with the car bodies only partly hidden by a sagging tin fence. Then up a hill, and past the gates to a gravel pit, which was a great cavity in the centre of the hill.

"That's them. That's their mailbox up ahead," Helen called out with some importance, and when they got close enough, she read out the name. "Matt and June Bergson. That's them."

26

A couple of dogs came barking down the short drive. One was large and black and one small and tan-coloured, puppy-like. They bumbled around at the wheels and Neal sounded the horn. Then another dog—this one more sly and purposeful, with a slick coat and bluish spots—slid out of the long grass.

Helen called to them to shut up, to lie down, to piss off. "You don't need to bother about any of them but Pinto," she said. "Them other two's just cowards."

They stopped in a wide, ill-defined space, where some gravel had been laid down. On one side was a barn or implement shed, tin covered, and over to one side of it, on the edge of a cornfield, an abandoned farmhouse. The house inhabited nowadays was a trailer, nicely fixed up with a deck and an awning, and a flower garden behind what looked like a toy fence. The trailer and its garden looked proper and tidy, while the rest of the property was littered with things that might have a purpose or might just have been left around to rust or rot.

Helen had jumped out and was cuffing the dogs. But they kept on running past her, and jumping and barking at the car, until a man came out of the shed and called to them. The threats and names he called were not intelligible to Jinny, but the dogs quieted down.

Jinny put on her hat. All this time, she had been holding it in her hand.

"They just got to show off," said Helen. Neal had got out, too, and was negotiating with the dogs in a resolute way. The man from the shed came toward them. He wore a purple T-shirt that was wet with sweat, clinging to his chest and stomach. He was fat enough to have breasts, and you could see his navel pushing out like a pregnant woman's.

27

Neal went to meet him with his hand out. The man slapped his own hand on his work pants, laughed, and shook Neal's. Jinny could not hear what they said. A woman came out of the trailer and opened the toy gate and latched it behind her.

"Muriel went and forgot she was supposed to bring my shoes," Helen called to her. "I phoned her up and everything, but she went and forgot anyway, so Mr. Lockley brought me out to get them."

The woman was fat, too, though not as fat as her husband. She wore a pink muumuu with Aztec suns on it, and her hair was streaked with gold. She moved across the gravel with a composed and hospitable air. Neal turned and introduced himself, then brought her to the car and introduced Jinny.

"Glad to meet you," the woman said. "You're the lady that isn't very well?"

"I'm okay," said Jinny.

"Well, now you're here, you better come inside. Come in out of this heat."

The man had come closer. "We got the air-conditioning in there," he said. He was inspecting the car, and his expression was genial but disparaging.

"We just came to pick up the shoes," Jinny said.

"You got to do more than that, now you're here," said the woman, June, laughing as if the idea of their not coming in was a scandalous joke. "You come in and rest yourselves."

"We wouldn't like to disturb your supper," Neal said.

"We had it already," said Matt. "We eat early."

"But there's all kinds of chili left," said June. "You have to come in and help clean up that chili."

Jinny said, "Oh, thank you. But I don't think I could eat

anything. I don't feel like eating anything when it's this hot."

"Then you better drink something, instead," June said. "We got ginger ale, Coke. We got peach schnapps."

"Beer," Matt said to Neal. "You like a Blue?"

Jinny waved at Neal, asking him to come close to her window. "I can't do it," she said. "Just tell them I can't."

"You know you'll hurt their feelings," he whispered. "They're trying to be nice."

"But I can't."

He bent closer. "You know what it looks like if you don't."

"You go."

"You'd be okay once you got inside. The air-conditioning really would do you good."

Jinny just shook her head.

Neal straightened up.

"Jinny thinks she better just stay in the car and rest here in the shade," Neal said. "But I wouldn't mind a Blue, actually."

He turned back to Jinny with a hard smile. He seemed to her desolate and angry. "You sure you'll be okay?" he said for the others to hear. "Sure? You don't mind if I go in for a little while?"

"I'll be fine," said Jinny.

He put one hand on Helen's shoulder and one on June's shoulder, walking them companionably toward the trailer. Matt smiled at Jinny curiously, and followed. This time, when he called the dogs to come after him, Jinny could make out their names.

Goober. Sally. Pinto.

The car was parked under a row of willow trees. These trees

were big and old, but their leaves were thin and gave a wavering shade. Still, to be alone was a great relief.

Earlier today, driving along the highway from the town where they lived, they had stopped at a roadside stand and bought some early apples. Jinny got one out of the bag at her feet and took a small bite—more or less to see if she could taste and swallow it and hold it in her stomach. It was all right. The apple was firm and tart, but not too tart, and if she took small bites and chewed seriously she could manage it.

She'd seen Neal like this—or something like this—a few times before. It would be over some boy at the school. A mention of the name in an offhand, even belittling way. A mushy look, an apologetic yet somehow defiant bit of giggling. But that was never anybody she had to have around the house, and it could never come to anything. The boy's time would be up, he'd go away.

So would this time be up. It shouldn't matter. She had to wonder if it would have mattered less yesterday than it did today.

She got out of the car, leaving the door open so that she could hang on to the inside handle. Anything on the outside was too hot to hang on to for any length of time. She had to see if she was steady. Then she walked a little, in the shade. Some of the willow leaves were already going yellow. Some were already lying on the ground. She looked out from the shade at all the things in the yard.

A dented delivery van with both headlights gone and the name on the side painted out. A baby's stroller that the dogs had chewed the seat out of, a load of firewood dumped but not stacked, a pile of huge tires, a great number of plastic jugs and some oil cans and pieces of old lumber and a couple of orange plastic tarpaulins crumpled up by the wall of the shed. What a lot of things people could find themselves in charge of. As Jinny had been in charge of all those photographs, official letters, minutes of meetings, newspaper clippings, a thousand categories that she had devised and had been putting on disk when she had to go into chemo and everything got taken away. All those things might end up being thrown out. As all this might, if Matt died.

The cornfield was the place she wanted to get to. The corn was higher than her head now, maybe higher than Neal's head—she wanted to get into the shade of it. She made her way across the yard with this one thought in mind. The dogs, thank God, must have been taken inside.

There was no fence. The cornfield just petered out into the yard. She walked straight ahead into it, onto the narrow path between two rows. The leaves flapped in her face and against her arms like streamers of oilcloth. She had to remove her hat, so they would not knock it off. Each stalk had its cob, like a baby in a shroud. There was a strong, almost sickening smell of vegetable growth, of green starch and hot sap.

What she had intended to do, once she got in there, was lie down. Lie down in the shade of these large, coarse leaves and not come out till she heard Neal calling her. Perhaps not even then. But the rows were too close together to permit that, and she was too busy thinking to take the trouble. She was too angry.

It was not about anything that had happened recently. She was remembering how a group of people had been sitting around one evening on the floor of her living-room —or meeting-room—playing one of those serious psychological games. One of those games that were supposed to make a person more honest and resilient. You had to say just what came into your mind as you looked at each of the others. And a white-haired woman named Addie Norton, a friend of Neal's, had said, "I hate to tell you this, Jinny, but whenever I look at you, all I can think of is—Nice Nelly."

Other people had said kinder things to her. "Flower child" or "Madonna of the Springs." She happened to know that whoever said that meant "Manon of the Springs," but she offered no correction. She was outraged at having to sit there and listen to people s opinions of her.

Everyone was wrong. She was not timid or acquiescent or natural or pure. When you died, of course, these wrong opinions were all that was left.

While this was going through her mind, she had done the easiest thing you can do in a cornfield—got lost. She had stepped over one row and then another, and probably got turned around. She tried going back the way she had come, but it obviously wasn't the right way. There were clouds over the sun again, so she couldn't tell where west was. And she had not checked which direction she was going when she entered the field, anyway, so that would not have helped. She stood still and heard nothing but the corn whispering away, and some distant traffic.

Her heart was pounding just like any heart that had years and years of life ahead of it.

Then a door opened, she heard the dogs barking and Matt yelling, and the door slammed shut. She pushed her way through stalks and leaves, in the direction of that noise. It turned out that she had not gone far at all. She had been stumbling around in one small corner of the field, the whole time.

Matt waved at her and warned off the dogs.

"Don't be scairt of them, don't be scairt," he called. He was going toward the car just as she was, though from another direction. As they got closer to each other, he spoke in a lower, perhaps more intimate, voice.

"You shoulda come and knocked on the door." He thought that she had gone into the corn to have a pee. "I just told your husband I'd come out and make sure you're okay."

Jinny said, "I'm fine. Thank you." She got into the car but left the door open. He might be insulted if she closed it. Also, she felt too weak.

"He was sure hungry for that chili."

Who was he talking about?

Neal.

She was trembling and sweating and there was a hum in her head, as if a wire were strung between her ears.

"I could bring you some out if you'd like it."

She shook her head, smiling. He lifted up the bottle of beer in his hand—he seemed to be saluting her.

"Drink?"

She shook her head again, still smiling.

"Not even a drink of water? We got good water here."

"No, thanks." If she turned her head and looked at his purple navel, she would gag.

"You hear about this fellow going out the door with a jar of horseradish in his hand?" he said in a changed voice. "And his dad says to him, 'Where you goin' with that horseradish?'

"'Going to get a horse,' he says.

"Dad says, 'You're not goin' to catch a horse with no horseradish.'

"Fellow comes back next morning. Nice big horse on a halter. Puts it in the barn.

"Next day Dad sees him goin' out, bunch of branches in his hand.

33

"'What's them branches in your hand?'

"'Them's pussy willows—'"

"What are you telling me this for?" Jinny said, almost shaking. "I don't want to hear it. It's too much."

"What's the matter now?" Matt said. "All it is is a joke."

Jinny was shaking her head, squeezing her hand over her mouth.

"Never mind," he said. "I won't take no more of your time."

He turned his back on her, not even bothering to call to the dogs.

"I do not wish to give the wrong impression or get carried away with optimism." The doctor had spoken in a studious, almost mechanical way. "But it looks as if we have a significant shrinkage. What we hoped for, of course. But frankly, we did not expect it. I do not mean that the battle is over. But we can be to a certain extent optimistic and proceed with the next course of chemo and see how things look then."

What are you telling me this for? I don't want to hear it. It's too much.

Jinny had not said anything like that to the doctor. Why should she? Why should she behave in such an unsatisfactory and ungrateful way, turning his news on its head? Nothing was his fault. But it was true that what he had said made everything harder. It made her have to go back and start this year all over again. It removed a certain low-grade freedom. A dull, protecting membrane that she had not even known was there had been pulled away and left her raw.

Matt's thinking she had gone into the cornfield to pee had

made her realize that she actually wanted to. Jinny got out of the car, stood cautiously, and spread her legs and lifted her wide cotton skirt. She had taken to wearing big skirts and no panties this summer, because her bladder was no longer under perfect control.

A dark stream trickled away from her through the gravel. The sun was down now. Evening was coming on, and there was a clear sky overhead. The clouds were gone.

One of the dogs barked half-heartedly, to say that somebody was coming but somebody they knew. They had not come over to bother her when she got out of the car—they were used to her now. They went running out to meet whoever it was, without any alarm or excitement.

It was a boy, or young man, riding a bicycle. He swerved toward the car and Jinny went round to meet him, a hand on the warm fender to support herself. When he spoke to her, she did not want it to be across her puddle. And maybe to distract him from even looking on the ground for such a thing, she spoke first. She said, "Hello. Are you delivering something?"

He laughed, springing off the bike and dropping it to the ground, all in one motion.

"I live here," he said. "I'm just getting home from work."

She thought that she should explain who she was, tell him how she came to be here and for how long. But all this was too difficult. Hanging on to the car like this, she must look like somebody who had just come out of a wreck.

"Yeah, I live here," he said. "But I work in a restaurant in town. I work at Sammy's."

A waiter. The bright-white shirt and black pants were waiters' clothes. And he had a waiter's air of patience and alertness.

"I'm Jinny Lockley," she said. "Helen. Helen is—"

35

"Okay, I know," he said. "You're who Helen's going to work for. Where's Helen?"

"In the house."

"Didn't nobody ask you in, then?"

He was about Helen's age, she thought. Seventeen or eighteen. Slim and graceful and cocky, with an ingenuous enthusiasm that would probably not get him as far as he hoped. Jinny had seen a few like that who ended up as Young Offenders. He seemed to understand things, though. He seemed to understand that she was exhausted and in some kind of muddle.

"June in there, too?" he said. "June's my mom."

His hair was coloured like June's, gold streaks over dark. He wore it rather long, and parted in the middle, flopping off to either side.

"Matt, too?" he said.

"And my husband. Yes."

"That's a shame."

"Oh, no," she said. "They asked me. I said I'd rather wait out here."

Neal used sometimes to bring home a couple of his Yo-yos, to be supervised doing lawn work or painting or basic carpentry. He thought it was good for them, to be accepted into somebody's home. Jinny had flirted with them occasionally, in a way that she could never be blamed for. Just a gentle tone, a way of making them aware of her soft skirts and her scent of apple soap. That wasn't why Neal had stopped bringing them. He had been told it was out of order.

"So how long have you been waiting?"

"I don't know," Jinny said. "I don't wear a watch."

"Is that right?" he said. "I don't, either. I don't hardly ever meet another person that doesn't wear a watch. Did you never wear one?"

She said, "No. Never."

"Me neither. Never, ever. I just never wanted to. I don't know why. Never, ever wanted to. Like, I always just seem to know what time it is anyway. Within a couple minutes. Five minutes at the most. Sometimes one of the diners asks me, 'Do you know the time,' and I just tell them. They don't even notice I'm not wearing a watch. I go and check as soon as I can, clock in the kitchen. But I never once had to go in there and tell them any different."

"I've been able to do that, too, once in a while," Jinny said. "I guess you do develop a sense, if you never wear a watch."

"Yeah, you really do."

"So what time do you think it is now?"

He laughed. He looked at the sky.

"Getting close to eight. Six, seven minutes to eight? I got an advantage, though. I know when I got off of work, and then I went to get some cigarettes at the 7-Eleven, and then I talked to some guys a couple of minutes, and then I hiked home. You don't live in town, do you?"

Jinny said no.

"So, where do you live?"

She told him.

"You getting tired? You want to go home? You want me to go in and tell your husband you want to go home?"

"No. Don't do that," she said.

"Okay, okay. I won't. June's probably telling their fortunes in there anyway. She can read hands."

"Can she?"

"Sure. She goes in the restaurant a couple of times a week. Tea, too. Tea leaves."

He picked up his bike and wheeled it out of the way of

the car. Then he looked in, through the driver's window.

"Keys in the car," he said. "So—you want me to drive you home or what? Your husband can get Matt to drive him and Helen when they get ready. And he can bring me back from your place. Or if it don't look like Matt can, June can. June's my mom, but Matt's not my dad. You don't drive, do you?"

"No," said Jinny. She had not driven for months.

"No. I didn't think so. Okay then? You want me to? Okay?"

"This is just a road I know. It'll get you there as soon as the highway."

They had not driven past the subdivision. In fact, they had headed the other way, taking a road that seemed to circle the gravel pit. At least they were going west now, toward the brightest part of the sky. Ricky—that was what he'd told her his name was—had not yet turned the car lights on.

"No danger meeting anybody," he said. "I don't think I ever met a single car on this road, ever. See—not so many people even know this road is here. And if I was to turn the lights on, then the sky would go dark, and everything would go dark, and you wouldn't be able to see where you were. We just give it a little while more, so then when it gets dark, we can see the stars, that's when we turn the lights on."

The sky was like very faintly coloured glass—red or yellow or green or blue glass, depending on which part of it you looked at. The bushes and trees would turn black, once the lights were on. There would just be black clumps along the road and the black mass of trees crowding in behind them, instead of, as now, the individual, still identifiable, spruce and cedar and feathery tamarack, and the jewelweed with its flowers like winking bits of fire. It seemed close enough to touch, and they were going slowly. She put her hand out.

Not quite. But close. The road seemed hardly wider than the car.

She thought she saw the gleam of a full ditch ahead. "Is there water down there?" she said.

"Down there?" said Ricky. "Down there and everywhere. There's water to both sides of us and lots of places, water underneath us. Want to see?"

He slowed the car down and stopped. "Look down your side," he said. "Open the door and look down."

When she did that, she saw that they were on a bridge. A little bridge, no more than ten feet long, of crosswise-laid planks. No railings. And motionless water.

"Bridges all along here," he said. "And where it's not bridges it's culverts. 'Cause it's always flowing back and forth under the road. Or just laying there and not flowing."

"How deep?" she said.

"Not deep. Not this time of year. Not till we get to the big pond—it's deeper. And then, in spring, it's all over the road, you can't drive here, it's deep then. This road goes flat for miles and miles, and it goes from one end to the other. There isn't even any road that cuts across it. This is the only road I know of through the Borneo Swamp."

Jinny said, "Borneo Swamp? There is an island called Borneo. It's halfway round the world."

"I don't know about that. All I ever heard of was just the Borneo Swamp."

There was a strip of dark grass now, growing down the middle of the road.

"Time for the lights," he said. He switched them on, and

39

they were in a tunnel in the sudden night. "Once I turned the lights on like that, and there was this porcupine. It was just sitting there in the middle of the road, sitting up on its hind legs, and looking right at me. Like some little tiny old man. It was scared to death and it couldn't move. I could see its little old teeth chattering."

Jinny thought, This is where he brings his girls.

"So what do I do? I tried beeping the horn, and it still didn't do nothing. I didn't feel like getting out and chasing it. He was scared, but he still was a porcupine and he could let fly. So I just parked there. I had time. When I turned the lights on again, he was gone." Now the branches really did reach the car and brush against the door, but if there were flowers she could not see them.

"I am going to show you something," he said. "I'm going to show you something like I bet you never seen before."

If this had been happening back in her old, normal life, it's possible that she might now have begun to be frightened. If she were back in her old, normal life she would not be here at all.

"You're going to show me a porcupine," she said.

"Nope. Not that."

A few miles farther on, he turned off the lights. "See the stars?" he said. He stopped the car. Everywhere, there was at first a deep silence. Then this silence was filled in, at the edges, by some kind of humming that could have been far-away traffic, and little noises that passed before you properly heard them, that could have been made by birds or bats or night-feeding animals.

"Come in here in the springtime," he said, "you wouldn't hear nothing but the frogs. You'd think you were going deaf with the frogs." He opened the door on his side.

"Now. Get out and walk a ways with me."

40

She did as she was told. She walked in one of the wheel tracks, he in the other. The sky seemed to be lighter ahead, and there was a different sound—something like mild and rhythmical conversation. The road turned to wood and the trees on either side were gone.

"Walk out on it," he said. "Go on."

He came close and touched her waist, guiding her. Then he took his hand away, left her to walk on these planks, which were like the deck of a boat. Like the deck of a boat, they rose and fell. But it wasn't a movement of waves, it was their footsteps, his and hers, that caused this rising and falling of the boards beneath them. "Now do you know where you are?" he said.

"On a dock?" she said.

"On a bridge. This is a floating bridge."

Now she could make it out—the plank roadway just a few inches above the still water. He drew her over to the side, and they looked down. There were stars riding on the water.

"It's dark all the time," he said proudly. "That's because it's a swamp. It's got the same stuff in it tea has got, and it looks like black tea."

She could see the shoreline, and the reed beds. Water in the reeds, lapping water, was what was making that sound.

"Tannin," she said.

The slight movement of the bridge made her imagine that all the trees and the reed beds were set on saucers of earth and the road was a floating ribbon of earth and underneath it all was water.

It was at this moment that she realized she didn't have her hat. She not only didn't have it on, she hadn't had it with her in the car. She had not been wearing it when she got out of the car to pee and when she began to talk to

41

Ricky. She had not been wearing it when she sat in the car with her head back against the seat and her eyes closed, when Matt was telling his joke. She must have dropped it in the cornfield, and in her panic left it there.

While she had been scared of seeing the mound of Matt's navel with the purple shirt plastered over it, he had been looking at her bleak knob.

"It's too bad the moon isn't up yet," Ricky said. "It's really nice here when the moon is up."

"It's nice now, too."

He slipped his arms around her as if there were no question at all about what he was doing and he could take all the time he wanted to do it. He kissed her mouth. It seemed to her that this was the first time that she had ever participated in a kiss that was an event in itself. The whole story, all by itself. A tender prologue, an efficient pressure, a whole-hearted probing and receiving, a lingering thanks, and a drawing away satisfied.

"Oh," he said. "Oh."

He turned her around, and they walked back the way they had come.

"So was that the first you ever been on a floating bridge?"

She said yes, it was.

He took her hand and swung it as if he would like to toss it.

"And that's the first time I ever kissed a married woman."

"You'll probably kiss a lot more of them," she said. "Before you're done."

He sighed. "Yeah," he said. "Yeah, I probably will."

Amazed, sobered, by the thought of his future.

She had a sudden thought of Neal, back on dry land. Neal also startled by the thought of the future, giddy and besotted and disbelieving, as he opened his hand to the gaze of the woman with bright streaks in her hair.

Jinny felt a rain of compassion, almost like laughter. A swish of tender hilarity, getting the better of her sores and hollows, for the time given.

An Apology

Ramona Dearing

The first day of the trial will be the hardest. Gerard Lundrigan arrives at the courthouse exactly one hour early, at nine o'clock. Even then the TV cameras are waiting, although they're not allowed inside the courtroom. He sits in that dark sanctuary, testing his chair. It will do. He's brought along the Graham Greene book he forgot to return to the library. But he can't read about the whiskey priest, not just yet. Gerard makes sure the buttons on his blue cardigan are done up right. He holds the book open so it will look like he's doing something. Outside the tall windows, what looks to be the start of a March storm. He'd forgotten what it was like here. The wind is taking anything it can find. There's a good chance that by noon all of St. John's will be clamped in ice. Or it will be sunny, or raining, or snowing. You never knew about this place, he does remember that. He thinks about his pup back in Ontario, and how it likes to nose through the snow. It would like it here, especially rolling in landwash after chasing gulls.

The jurors look nervous as they walk in. One woman giggles when she bumps into a chair on the way to the jury box, and her face stays red for a full hour. The other jurors' eyes swivel over the oak and mahogany scrollings, the ancient picture of the Queen, the thin, bunned judge in her red-sashed blue robe. A sheriff's officer walks around with one hand pressed to his earpiece, the other clamped at his hip to keep the keys on his belt from jingling. Two more sheriff's officers flank Gerard, tapping their fingers against their thighs. There can be trouble on the first day, apparently, scenes. The lawyers look edgy and clear their throats a lot. Gerard isn't sure how many spectators there are—he won't let himself look back. But there are eyes on him, of course—he can feel them. And he can see the jurors studying him. They've relaxed a bit, are sitting more deeply in their chairs. Not one of them looks like a leader. Not one of them looks to be well-studied. Only one man wears a tie. There's even a girl in jeans, chewing gum. They listen hard as the crown prosecutor outlines his case. During the preliminary inquiry, he'd been soft-spoken, methodical. Now he is playing to the jury, and there is insincerity and filth coming out his mouth. Absolute filth.

You're probably nervous, ladies and gentlemen of the jury. I know you are because I myself am nervous right now and I've been at this racket for a long time now. But there's no need to worry. All you have to do is sort through the facts, and I believe those facts are very clearly set out. You are the judge of the facts and as such, you will hear direct testimony that Brother Lundrigan beat little boys. Sodomized little boys. Ejaculated in their mouths as they gagged and struggled.

You will hear these allegations from eleven different men. The trial is expected to take six weeks.

Most of the jurors suction their arms across their stomachs and keep them there all morning. Gerard sits very tall and looks straight ahead.

The afternoon is better. The weather has settled somewhat. The first witness is called—the lead investigator from the Royal Newfoundland Constabulary. All he does is show a videotape of the orphanage, a long, long tape showing every room and closet and corridor and shed. The police shot the film before the wrecking ball knocked the place in on itself. There is the chapel, just as Gerard remembers it. The class-rooms. The sleeping quarters. The gym. The old garden grounds. And so on, and on and on. All shot poorly, shak-ily, with bad lighting. But the courtroom has been dark-ened and therefore no-one is staring at Gerard.

When the first complainant takes the stand, Gerard absorbs every word. He remembers the boy well. The one who'd wanted so badly to be on the gymnastics team but was disqualified because he failed math every year. He'd been a big boy then. Now he has the look of a withered drunk. Ridiculous in a burgundy velvet jacket. Soft-spoken—the judge doesn't ask the man to speak up nearly enough. He didn't get that mumbling habit from his time at the or-phanage. They'd taught pride there. Pride and decency and right-living.

The fellow goes on for hours about how terrible the orphanage was, how he and his younger brother would steal buns and hide them in the little barn for the times when they couldn't sleep for hunger. How they got in trouble just for sitting still, and worse beatings when they actually did anything bad. How Bro. Lundrigan was the worst one for the strap, especially with the boys in his dorm. How he wouldn't tolerate any illness and wouldn't let a boy go to the sickroom even if he'd thrown up all night. How Bro. Lundrigan would toss any boy who wet the bed into the swimming-pool. How if he saw a boy crying for any reason,

46

he'd rub soap in the child's eyes so he'd have something to screech about.

Gerard wants to speak. It's physically painful not to be able to respond, acid burning his gut. But since he won't be testifying for at least a month, he's started a notebook outlining every single point he disagrees with, numbering each in case it will help his lawyer.

23) No child ever went hungry in my care.

24) The strap had nothing to do with me. Blame the era, not the man. Do you think your disobedience made me happy—do you think I liked it?

25) I remember personally taking you to the sickroom on at least two occasions.

26) Re: soap—whatever are you talking about?

"Make him stop watching me," the first complainant says to the judge the fifth morning he's on the stand. The prosecutor has just started in on the buggery allegations. On the fire escape, one night. In the barn, many times. Many, many times. The witness's voice cracks. The judge orders a break.

117) The disgusting thing you allude to—where would I even have gotten the idea? What about my vows? Why would I do such a thing? You brought me here to watch your sickening tears and listen to you say these revolting things?

Gerard is thankful for his lawyer, who establishes in one efficient afternoon of cross-examination that the complainant has a long criminal record, including theft. He'd also attacked a man in a bar with a broken bottle. That's the kind of low-life he is. In and out of mental hospitals, with children spat out across Northern Ontario like bits of gristle, and ex-wives lining up to get restraining orders.

The next witness is a real crowd-pleaser. Makes the jury smile as he remembers stringing chestnuts to play conkers. As he describes skinning his shins against the rough concrete of the swimming-pool. The time Bro. Superior came in for breakfast one morning dressed like Charlie Chaplin and kept pretending to fall off his chair. What it was like riding the hay wagon into St. John's and seeing all those mesmerizing lights and the houses where you could look in the windows at the moms and dads and pops and nannies and little kids sitting right nice and sweet at the table.

He has them all right. Even the judge looks choked up. And then less than half an hour later, he goes for a bull's-eye. His face is crazy red and he's dry-sobbing and beating one hand against the top of the witness box and pointing with the other: *That one, that one there. That bastard ruined me for everything. Your Honour, I'd as soon spit on him on his deathbed. That's a monster, that is. Not a man. Left me opened up and bleeding so's I couldn't shit for a week. Bite marks on my neck.*

The judge orders a break.

Gerard has begun to put together some theories. These men are 45, 50. They're all into the booze or the drugs. They've all done time. He knows—it all came out at the preliminary hearing.

They've got something else in common: they've disappointed anyone who ever came into their lives. Including Gerard.

Their fathers were alcoholics or thieves or dead and their mothers were sluts or mad or dead. Now they're men looking to blame, to make someone accountable for their empty spots.

And who better than Gerard? They remember him

making them sit on their bleeding hands—as was common in those times—and they want revenge, they want to make him sit on his own bleeding hands and get a taste of himself. They'd do that to a 64-year-old because all they want is this one chance in their lives to give out orders and have someone obey.

So, okay, Gerard is sitting on his hands. They've got him where they want him. They wag their fingers like he used to in math class, and now it's him who can't talk back. It's so straightforward eye-for-an-eye that it's almost comic. Except what they really want is for him to fix their lives and that's something he never, ever could do.

A man is not a mother. A 22-year old thinks he wants to get away from his slightly aristocratic parents. He thinks he wants to roll up his sleeves, get his hands dirty, serve. And so he does. And at first, God is everywhere. In the wind, in his ear, in the fellowship of the 23-year-olds and the 25-year-olds who also want nothing of society auctions and marriage and cigars. But there are fourteen boys in his charge. Two are just four years old, leggy babies with permanent ropes of snot hanging from their noses. Crying always for Mamma. The teen boys are revolting, with their acne and their smell and their trembling beds as they go at themselves in the dark. The middle ones are better, but still they hang off him, one on one arm, another on his back, another trying to get that one off. *Possums*, he'd called them, but he had to explain: no possums in Newfoundland.

Ripped off. Yes, they were. He always knew that. It was not easy for them. But it wasn't easy for him, either. Does anyone ever stop and think what it was like? Up at 5.30 for prayers with the other brothers. Getting the boys up at six and trying to get them to wash. Supervising breakfast. Teaching until four. Gymnastics coaching. Homework

49

supervision. Somewhere in there making time to go over to the teachers' dorm and help out with the bed-bound ancient brothers. Then supervising his dorm, staying up all night if necessary with the croupy boys.

And those annual evaluations with the superior. Always getting on about the filth of the place, about how the boys needed to be pushed to do their chores properly. The lavatory like something out of India. How Bro. Superior wanted things pristine, the way they should be. And how the orphanage should be winning more trophies—how good it was for the boys to be the very best, to show them that adversity could be overcome.

One time Gerard muttered under his breath *Yes, Bro., but what about my needs?* It had struck him as funny—by rights he'd prayed them all away hadn't he? That wasn't so long before he'd left. He remembers it was a Tuesday, and he'd walked back over to the main building and announced to all the boys at supper that there'd be no homework that night. They'd see *Gold Rush* instead and each boy could go to the canteen and pick out chips and a soda and a bar. All evening he felt naughty and proud. But he tossed and turned in bed, worried he'd acted out of false pride.

After the third man takes the stand, Gerard decides he can't keep thinking about the past. What good does it do, dredging up these old details? He's got things happening in his life right now that need attention, and all because of this trial. His lawyer has told him to keep taking notes. But everything that is being said has been already been said twice before and presumably will go around nine more times. The jurors are starting to look bored. They get sent out of the courtroom a lot while the lawyers argue whether certain lines of questioning should be allowed. Gerard has heard the sheriff's officers say the women are knitting up a storm during the time they wait downstairs in the jury-room and that one of them brought in this cappuccino machine they're all going mad for.

The lawyers have settled into a steadiness, a matter-of-factness. It has been seven weeks now. They joke about being here for another three months.

Here I am just a bit taller than the door latch—I can feel it digging in back of my head—and here he is picking me up by my ears and telling me to clamp it or everything is going to hurt more.

More and more, all Gerard can think of is the pup and how it's doing. He remembers the little squeaky sound it makes when it yawns. He doesn't know why he got it with the trial coming up, but he did. He wasn't going to, but then the trial was postponed for the second time, some conflict with the judge's schedule. He just saw the pup—in a pet store, of all places—and took it home.

He'd felt like a new mother. Every sound led back to the pup. He was in the library one day when he was sure he could hear Brigus keening. Gerard had stood there waiting for claws to scrape white lines on his shins. But of course the dog wasn't there. The sound must have been a pencil sharpener or some such thing.

Walking home the long way, the pretty way—along the Avon and its low-waisted willows, past Tom Patterson Island, past the Stratford Festival Theatre, past the squirrels —another squeal from Brigus, except really it came from a gull. And the next false alarm was a scream of brakes from a bus.

When he'd returned home to the pup, a copy of *The Power and the Glory* warming his armpit, there was only the sound of his keys hitting the table and a metronome of tail hitting the sides of the crate. Thump thump thump thump, etc.

I never told no-one until my lady put it on the line. She said, "Look, my honey, you've got something eating you all these years and it's eating me too and I'm falling apart and I don't even know why."

He wonders how the housesitter is making out. He calls her a couple of times a week and she says everything's fine, but he wonders if that's really the case. It bothers him, having someone in his house. But what can he do? The pup can't be abandoned.

He'd put an ad in the paper for a caretaker. The girl answered and so did some older women and a boy maybe 21. He interviewed the boy and liked him best, but decided against him on the basis of the trouble factor with boys. The women talked too much. The girl was quiet. He had her move in the week before he left just to make sure he could trust her. She didn't spend any time on the phone, which surprised him. She washed her dishes as soon as she finished eating. She spent all her time with the pup, mostly outside.

He'd told her he didn't know how long he'd be gone on business. Depended how the deal went. Not too long, he didn't think.

"You still working?" It was the only question she ever asked him. He'd nodded. At night, he could hear her drag the nightstand up against her door. She kept the pup in with her.

I said, "Lord Jesus, take me out of this." And then I tried with the razor. I really wanted it. I would picture Bro. Lundrigan walking past my casket getting all shaky.

Okay, he's not a saint. There are times he's picked Brigus up by the scruff and shaken him and whacked him, once even in front of the girl. You can only trip down the stairs so many times with fifteen pounds of stupidity skinning

52

your heel. You can only pick up gummed toilet paper so many times off the living-room floor, say goodbye to so many boots and tea-towels. Gerard had taken to reading a book on dog training by some monks who raise and sell drug-sniffing German Shepherds at their monastery in New York State. He'd read it at 4.30 in the morning, wide awake after taking the dog outside for its first shit of the day. While Gerard read, Brigus would curl tight, a potato bug on the floor next to the bedframe. The monks say to never give in to exasperation. Stay in control. *To stop biting, give the snout a firm but harmless shake. Expect a yelp of surprise. Hold the palm flat and ask for a lick instead. Praise your pup.* Sometimes Gerard has grabbed the pup's snout just to make it cry out.

Brigus never seems to bite the girl. She's to dust and vacuum and scrub every week. No visitors. She'll be needing to keep the lawn cut and the garden tidy. "You understand everything I'm paying you to do?" he'd said. She'd nodded. It was his parents' house, he told her, and needed to be treated with that kind of respect. She'd nodded again. The pup was to be her first priority, though. Another nod, this time with a slight smile attached.

He wonders if she's having parties. If there are people fornicating in his house right now. In his parents' old bed. He decides to call again at the lunch break.

No answer, for the fourth day in a row.

The fifth complainant knocks the hell out of him. Gerard has no idea who he is. He knows he didn't recognize the name, but he thought when he saw the fellow it would all click. The man hadn't been at the prelim, and now that Gerard is finally looking right at him, he can't place him at all.

At lunch he says to his lawyer, "How could I not know one of the children?"

His lawyer looks tired. "What's to remember when you're dealing with a liar?"

The records point to Gerard teaching the man for three years—he apparently failed Grade 7 math. He's convinced the man must have had another name back then. How could Gerard forget one of the boys?

The lack of giving in the dog really surprised him. He wishes he could talk to the New York State monks about that. They'd know what he means. It sits there insisting on being noticed, forever complaining. Something the orphans never would have dared. Fat Brigus, ears flopping back and forth as he pisses on the bathmat, wants chicken, wrestling matches, lap-naps and cheese.

Surely the dog will still know him when he gets back?

He remembers the eleventh complainant in great detail. A sweet boy he was, needy but still sweet. Had these fat ringlets and a long skinny frame. Gerard's favourite possum, always leaning in, content. *Look what I got you, Brother.* And in his fist a wet stone, one side glowing an ashy red if the light hit it right. Gerard would pick him up and hold him tight.

He's grey now and has his hair clipped. Still thin, though. He would have loved Brigus, that boy, would have petted him bald. *If you pinches the pads on their feet they won't jump up no more, isn't that right? You gots to give them a big squirt of a squeeze whenever they does that. Can I touch his tail, Brother? I mean, may I, Bro.?*

The mother of the eleventh man gets herself in the paper.

54

Apparently she's been in the public gallery through the whole trial. She waits until her boy's finished testifying. He has been crying softly for the last hour or so on the stand. But the mother doesn't go to her son. No, as soon as the judge leaves the courtroom, she walks up behind Gerard and tugs on the elbow of his cardigan and explains who she is.

No-one else has spoken to him, aside from his lawyer. The reporters look down when he walks past them. The sheriff's officers never speak directly to him. "Does Mr. Lundrigan want some water?" they'll ask his lawyer. The clerks don't look at him. Even in corner stores, if he's buying a paper or some chocolate, no-one looks right at him. Sometimes the cashier won't hold her hand out to take the money, forcing him to leave it on the counter and forget about the change.

But the mother smiles. "I've forgiven you," she says.

Gerard's lawyer moves closer.

"I've thought about it and you're going to do your time and you should get at least one more little chance, you know. I mean, who in frig am I to rebuke you? I mean, I'm the one who handed over my boy, right?"

The spectators who are getting ready to put on their coats are like hares, all ears and eyes.

The woman's voice is getting louder, too. "I kept saying he's just a man, same as any other. Just a man. That's how I'm going to look at you, anyway. Others might not, but I'm going to. For me, you know. For myself. Important, you know?"

Gerard turns from her, reaches for his coat.

She comes around on the other side so that she's still facing him. The reporters are there now, too, holding out microphones. "I mean nothing can give back my Sean what you took, so why should we keep after you, really? I mean, jail, yes. Go to jail for a while, you definitely should do that. But hatred, that's no good."

"Okay, okay," the sheriff's officers say. "This courtroom's closed for the day." They have their hands on her elbows and are edging her back, gently.

She says, "Do you have a message I could bring to the boys for you?"

He puts his arms across his chest and hates himself for doing it.

"Len Stamps, Red Matthews, Tom Walsh. You remember them all, right? Plus my Sean, of course."

The officers are getting her closer to the door. She's pushing against them.

"Donnie Hawko. Bill Wheaton, John Cooke, Vince Rutherford. You heard them. You heard what they said."

The reporters are following her, trying to ask her questions. But she ignores them.

"Say you're sorry," she yells. "Say 'I apologize.' Just say that. You'll feel better."

The next afternoon, Gerard is on the stand. The only witness for the defence. Some of the other Brothers wouldn't take the stand at their trials. But the juries didn't like that, apparently. Besides, Gerard doesn't mind talking. There's no way he can keep sitting on his hands.

The jury will see the authority he carries, the calm. The jury will remember the complainants and their mental illnesses, their criminal records. The roughness about them.

Except when he first gets on the stand, he feels like he might pass out. Everywhere he looks, he sees set faces.

He imagines the girl bringing Brigus here, coming in through the spectators' door and letting him off the lead at the back of the courtroom, a much bigger Brigus running at full hurl to cover Gerard with licks. He sees everyone smiling: the judge, the jury, the audience, himself.

After that, he gets his confidence back. *We wanted those boys to have a chance in the world. We pushed them. We made it clear everything was going to be hard for them. We didn't believe in pretending they weren't orphans.*

On the Sunday before cross-examination is to start, the girl answers the phone. She tells him she's seen his picture in the paper. She says she'll take care of the dog no matter what but she doesn't know if she can stay in the house because it is too sickening. She is thinking about going home to her parents and taking Brigus with her. "No," Gerard says. "You have to stay." If she leaves, she could steal everything on her way out. She could write things on the walls. She could set the house on fire. She could take Brigus and never give him back.

"Who exactly are you to be setting the rules?" she says, and he understands then her quietness is not as peaceful as he'd thought.

All he can say is, "Please, it's not whatever you're thinking." And offer extra money.

The crown attorney mocks him. "You mean, you taught this man for three years but can't remember him? Therefore, if you can't remember him, we're to conclude you're innocent? Okay, let's look at that. Let's say you couldn't remember whether you'd filed your income taxes for last year. Let's say it turns out you didn't. Does that mean, in the eyes of Revenue Canada, that you're off the hook, Mr. Lundrigan?"

Gerard can only repeat what he's already said several

times: "I know the records indicate that man was in my classroom three years running, but I also know I'd never laid eyes on him before this trial started, so how could I have done these terrible things as he claims?"

The jury finds that amusing. The judge calls a break.

There's another bad moment on what turns out to be Gerard's last day of cross-examination. It involves the allegations of the last complainant, Sean.

"Did you ever, Mr. Lundrigan, slip your tongue into his mouth as alleged?"

"No. But perhaps once when I kissed him there might have been an accident."

"You kissed the boy?"

"Yes, many times. Like a mother."

"On the lips?"

"Yes, sir. Like a mother would."

"Did you kiss the other boys?

"No, sir."

"Why not?"

"He was special, very dear to me, innocent. He needed affection."

"So you kissed him on the lips?"

"I've already answered that."

"Like a mother?"

"Like a mother."

"Did you ever insert your penis into his mouth?"

"Of course not."

"Even by accident?"

Gerard's lawyer objects, and the judge agrees. She calls an early lunch break.

Gerard's lawyer says he can't eat with him today—he has to run to the dentist. A weak lie since normally they'd still be in session.

Gerard sees Sean's mother putting on her coat in the last row of benches in the public gallery. He wouldn't let himself look over that way when he was on the stand. Now she won't look at him.

The judge gives her charge to the jury. It takes two days for her to finish. Gerard spends the time working on an apology to the boys, but nothing comes out right.

I have no malice toward you. You came to us robbed. We were only boys ourselves, you forget that.

I'm sorry you made me come here.

I'm sorry you've made such a fuss.

I'm sorry you want my blood.

To think he wiped their asses.

A pity his lawyer would never let him send a letter. It might help them.

The jury is out. Gerard's lawyer gives him a cell phone and tells him to stay within a ten-minute radius of the courtroom. The lawyer says not to fret if the deliberations take several days—the longer, the better. "I'd hang out with you," the lawyer says, "but I'm just snowballed with work at the office."

At first Gerard stays in the little apartment he's rented. He knew the wait was going to be bad, but not this bad. If he lies on the bed, the ceiling comes down to a point just above his nose. The more he paces, the more he sees himself in the mirrors that are all over the room. If he looks out the window, he feels lonely.

The harbour is quiet. The *Astron* is in, and a fisheries patrol vessel. Some longliners. It is sunny, and even better, it's windy. Somehow the gusts comfort him. It's a clean wind here, a wind that leaves the good in you.

It licks at him as he starts winding up the road to Signal Hill. Maybe no-one will recognize him with his ear flaps down. Not that he's hiding—it's the kind of cold that makes your eardrums ache.

The flags at Cabot Tower flap like tents in a blizzard. The few people walking around up here actually nod at him. It's a community of sorts, brought on by the elements.

He walks over to the Queen's Battery and looks down at Chain Rock. He could aim for it. There's no way he could even come close. But he could tell himself that's what he was doing. The wind would rub him against a rock face on the way down. If he waits until he's a bit colder he probably wouldn't feel a thing.

He remembers his last day with the dog. Not even that went right. He'd only meant to nudge Brigus toward the door with his foot but for some reason he'd kicked the pup good and hard. He'd spent forever trying to get it out from under the couch. In the end Gerard set up a semi-circle of cheese cubes, like stepping stones to the centre of the living-room.

Outside, they'd passed through the art gallery grounds to get down to the river. Brigus barrelled through the steel sculpture that looks like an oversized napkin holder and then spun around, checking to make sure he could still see Gerard. When they got over the railroad tracks and down the hill, the dog hacked after studiously and sombrely licking a mound of dirt. Gerard had felt like whipping himself. "I'm no good for you," he'd said, and walked away, fast. But no matter where he stepped, he could hear the pup rushing the grass right behind.

What you do and what you mean. Two entirely different

things. Gerard never meant anyone any trouble.

He does mean to push off right now, but he can't do it.

He heads down the footpath to the Interpretation Centre, where there are payphones—he's not allowed to tie up the cell phone. Gerard calls his house and, miraculously, the girl picks up.

"You're still there?" he says.

"I need the money, okay?"

"That's fine," he says, "I'm happy."

No response.

Gerard tries again. "He's your dog, okay? You take him. If you go."

The wind makes him cry on the way back down the hill. It keeps grinding bits of dirt right in there. He's hurrying because he's just now understanding it's not going to take the jury long.

There's so much wind he wonders whether he'll even hear the phone if it rings in his pocket.

But he does. He's surprised how relieved he feels.

Standing on Richards

George Bowering

Richards Street in downtown Vancouver is pretty interesting or pretty boring, depending on your point of view. Of all the people standing on corners along Richards Street, I am probably the only one who knows that it was named after Captain George Harry Richards, the nineteenth-century surveyor who gave False Creek its name.

Try it. Go up to one of the girls on the corner of Richards and, say, Nelson, and ask, "Hey, did you know that this street was named after the nineteenth-century surveyor who gave False Creek its name?"

"Oh, yeah, like I really give a shit about that." That's what she'll say.

Most nights I stand on the corner of Richards and Helmcken. Helmcken, by the way, was a Hudson's Bay Company doctor who made a lot of money on real estate around Victoria in the late nineteenth century. He was cosy with the Americans.

I dont look like anyone else standing on corners along Richards. You go down to Richards and Nelson and you get your tall young women in high heels. In the summer you can see the cheeks of their asses. In the winter they are nearly freezing because they might have winter coats, but they leave them open so guys in slowly cruising cars can see their long legs. An awful lot of them are blondes of one sort or another, because the Asian businessmen and tourists dont come all the way over here for women with dark hair.

I like Danielle. She has the darkest hair you ever saw, and she doesnt care. She's got eyes that could give a Japanese volleyball coach a heart attack. She's also got a Ph.D in anthropology. But when it came to selling, she decided to sell her body. I have nothing against her body.

That's a witticism.

I have nothing against her decision. As far as I can see, she's the only girl on Richards that had to make that choice.

A couple blocks in the other direction you'll see the boys and the young men trying to look like boys, around Richards and whatever that street is the other side of Davie. If you want to be one of those boys you have to be skinny. You have to look as if you could get hurt easily, and you have to know what to wear, no T-shirts with designer names on them, no No Fear, no Club Monaco. You dont want to be wearing a baseball cap backward. A nice clean pair of tans and a white shirt with some buttons undone will do the trick. You have to look as if you've done this before, just to be safe, and you have to look as if you havent been doing this for long. There arent any real stores or cafés down there past Davie, so you stand out like a sore you know what.

Usually I am the only person standing on the corner of Richards and Helmcken. Hardly anyone pronounces that name right. It is something like "Helmakin." Or it was when it was still attached to Dr. John S. Helmcken, the first doctor to show up in Victoria, in 1850. He married one of Governor Douglas's daughters and started buying up real estate. Doctors have been doing something like that ever since, except maybe the doctors who try to take care of the less lucky people standing on corners along Richards Street.

So I was going to tell you that I look somewhat different from the other people standing on corners along Richards. You wont see my bare legs, that's for certain, and I do not look in any way like a boy. I guess I look like a college professor from about twenty years ago. I'm wearing brown shoes, no sign of recent polishing, laces not as long as they used to be. Gabardine slacks, either dark brown or grey, I'm not sure. A light blue long-sleeve shirt with an ink stain at the bottom of the pocket, and a tie with stripes on a slant. One of those generic old school ties, somewhat wider than the ties I see salesmen wearing these days. Bifocal glasses that have frames halfway between round and square. And a genuine Harris tweed jacket.

Let me explain why I said "genuine." You see, first of all, a lot of people think that tweeds are called tweeds because they are woven in the Tweed Valley. Well, some of them are woven in the Tweed Valley, but that is not how we got the word tweed. Tweeds are made from varieties of the old twill weave, and the old Scottish word for twill is tweel. In 1826 some clerk in London made an understandable mistake, writing "tweed" instead of "tweel," and it was not long until our jackets were called tweeds, even in Scotland.

So what about Harris? Well, if you go across The Minch from the top of mainland Scotland, you will come to the biggest island in the Outer Hebrides. Stornaway Castle is up there, you may remember. Well, really it is all one island called Lewis Island, but the locals always refer to two islands, Lewis and Harris. No-one knows why, but it may be because Lewis is a lot hillier, or mountainous, as they say

64

over there. In any case, if someone had not started the Harris tweed cottage industry, they would have had to get by on fishing, and you know how unlikely that has become over the years.

So that's why I said "genuine." Harris tweeds are the most northerly tweeds, so the sheep they get the wool from have the thickest and toughest texture. That's my theory, anyway. If you are interested in a tweed jacket, have a good look at the label. Look for the word "genuine."

I said that I look like a professor from about twenty years ago. In fact I *was* a professor twenty years ago. I was a professor *five* years ago, professor of English. I was one of those strange ducks who kept reading outside my field of expertise. In fact, most people in my field of expertise, Nineteenth Century American Literature, knew a lot more about the recent work in the field than I did. I didnt want to stop reading Latin poetry and Japanese novels and provincial history, so I sort of fell behind in the latest theory about criticism of Nineteenth Century American prose and/or poetry. Every time I started to read some of the latest theory about criticism in my field of expertise, I would run into the word "hegemonic" or the word "template." So I would put the paper aside and pick up Plutarch.

But that is not the real reason I quit being a professor. Not the only one, anyway. I quit because I was finding it difficult to find anyone who wanted to know anything about literature. Once in a while I would have to supervise a graduate student who was interested in hegemonic templates in recent criticism of W.D. Howells, and I would encourage that young person to read *The Atlantic Monthly* from 1871 through 1881. But I was always tabbed to do more than my share of first-year English classes. An Introduction to English Fiction—that sort of thing.

Maybe there's something wrong with me. I still get all excited when I read an author I have never bothered with before, someone like, say, Mrs Chapone. Or when I find a new book about Fort Simpson and the Christian missionaries along the northern coast.

So you can imagine how I felt when September would slide into October, and it would become apparent that the youngsters in their backward caps and Club Monaco sweat-shirts didnt particularly want to learn anything. In fact more and more of them let it be known that once they had paid their tuition money they thought it was an imposition to make them read anything as well.

So I quit.

I wanted to see whether there was some place where I could sell my mind to someone who wanted to buy it.

I told this story to Danielle. She told me that she understood perfectly. She probably did. She never told me whether she had quit a professor job, or whether she had just got a Ph.D for the fun of it and didnt want to drive cab.

You might say who would stop their car and haggle over price with a guy in a tweed jacket who wants to sell his mind on Richards Street. I know I did. But I thought that I would give it a try. If that didnt work, there must be lots of other ways of selling your mind. Well, that's what I had been doing for twenty years at the university on the hill.

In recent years the university had acquired some high-rise space for a campus extension downtown, just off the financial district. Twenty-five tired students and I used to sit in a room with sealed windows every Tuesday night, two hours and a cigarette break and two more hours, not a coffee shop within walking distance because the business-men were all at home drinking vodka. Then I would walk up Howe Street, turn right on Georgia, turn right into a lane, and get into my professor car. Head home, have a last coffee, and lie in bed, trying to remember what I had to teach in the morning.

When you turned right at Georgia Street in those times, you walked past a number of tall young prostitutes trying to look upscale. One night after four hours of trying to get tired students interested in reading Henry James, I was walking past the genteel windows in front of the Georgia Hotel, when a good-looking young woman with glowing dark brown skin spoke to me.

"Would you like some company?"

She sounded cheerful.

"No thanks. I'm going to go home and read," I said, still walking.

"I'll read to you," she called out, as I turned in at the lane.

I did not change my pace, but I imagined, not for the last time, bringing that pleasant woman home to read to me. In a negligée, I guess. Say, hanging open in the front. One glowing breast peeking out, let's say.

So one sunny day in June I took along my old flaked briefcase and stood on the corner of Richards and Helmcken. I had books in the briefcase, and the first thing I did was to set the briefcase down and take out Margaret Ormsby's *British Columbia: a History*, and start reading. I would read a paragraph and then scan the windshields of slowly approaching cars for a bit, then bend my whitening head and read another paragraph. Ormsby's book was published in time for the province's centenary in 1858. Well, the province has had a number of centenaries. Some people, unaware of the difference between a noun and an adjective, call them centennials. These are no doubt the same people who thought that the new millennium would start in January 2000. I wonder why they didnt just call it the new millennial?

Anyway, it was not the first time I had read Ormsby's book, but it seemed to me that it would make good reading while I waited for someone to come along and buy an hour of my mind. I had a lot to learn about that. I was already well into Chapter 7, "Jewel in Queen Victoria's Diadem," before anyone stopped, and it was already past nine at night.

I had watched what the girls did. When the car came to a stop at the curb in front of me, I went over and bent down, first looking to check for possible violence, then at the open side window, for negotiation. A thirtyish guy with a balding forehead leaned over and asked me what the hell I was doing.

"I been driving by here ten times today, and you're always there," he said.

"Just about," I said, ready to add words about a late lunch and several pees.

"What the hell are you doing?"

"I'm—"

"What's with the book? Always the book."

"I guess two things. How can a person stand around all day without a book to read—"

"Do it all the—"

"And it's kind of what you might call public information. I mean I wouldnt want people to get the wrong idea," I said.

There was a cop car approaching, slowly. It crossed my mind that this guy I was talking to was also a cop, hoping to entrap me. Thank goodness, I thought, neither of us had mentioned anything about money. The cop on my side of their car looked me up and down. He did not smirk, just kept that blank look the cops favour. The cop car pulled away, changing lanes without signalling.

"What wrong idea?" asked my guy in the car.

"Ah, well, I mean, I wouldnt want anyone to think I was just some low-IQ person blessed with a desirable body."

"Har har," he said. It looked as if he were preparing to drive away.

But he was my first possible sale. I decided to turn on my special gift for patter, the talent that had kept me in the classroom for two decades without disaster.

"Har har indeed," I said.

"So what would be the right idea?"

"Well," I said, and made the throat sound that is often conveyed with the printed word "harrumph." "The other attractive people you see standing on corners up and down this street are seeking to sell, or rather rent, their bodies. I seek to sell or rent my mind."

"Hardy har har," he said, and drove away.

"Conrad car car," I said into the night, regretting that no-one within earshot would recognize the instant and multilevelled word play.

When I was an undergraduate, the English professors let it be known that while they had to teach Hardy and Conrad in the same course, they reserved most of their respect for Conrad. He anticipated the psychological insights that would animate the major novelists and poets and film-makers in the modern era, while Hardy was a typical Victorian with a ham-handed approach to characterization.

Secretly I had always preferred Hardy. He let you know how sad he was about the world. Conrad was interested in exhibiting moral conflicts, but you never got the sense that he cared all that much when his characters failed the test.

Hardy, though blessed with an arch sarcasm, would often turn the screws of fate so hard on his people that you wanted to lament the lack of justice in the mortal world.

I thought about Hardy and Conrad for hours rather than reading in the evening light that made its way through the three layers of cloud over Vancouver. I did not get another prospective client, though several cars slowed as they passed my corner. I tried to look intellectually seductive, which consisted mainly of fiddling with my old brier and looking over the top of my glasses.

When I quit teaching the university gave me the equivalent of two years' salary, which I banked and paid income tax on. I'm still pretty comfortable, though it will be over a decade till my pension kicks in. It was not out of financial desperation that I first stood on my corner. I suppose I may have needed something to fill my days now that I was no longer pretending to write my book on Matthew Arnold. But the main reason for my being there was a kind of curiosity. I wanted to know whether men who drove slowly down certain streets in downtown Vancouver were as lonely for knowledge as they were for physical spasms.

Maybe some of those people driving by in their slow quiet cars were just too bashful or too little experienced to stop and bargain for knowledge. Maybe they had been enucleated by the popular culture, as people these days were calling it. I am one of the few old codgers who would insist that by "culture" they mean such things as literature, serious music and the Quattrocento.

Danielle stopped to say hello on her way back from her coffee break at a shop next to the library. She was gorgeous in patent leather boots that zipped up to her thighs. She had a form-fitting jacket that seemed to be made principally of red egret feathers.

"Aubrey, how long are you going to carry out this feck-
less experiment?" she asked. "Why dont you go home, have
a nice chocolate Ovaltine and snuggle up with *The Decline
and Fall of the Roman Empire?*"

"I've read it four times. I know it off by heart."

"Aubrey, you're going to give Richards Street a bad
name," she said.

"Did you ever consider that I am hanging out here so
that I can gaze at you just a block away?"

"I charge $200 an hour for gazing, chum."

She gave me her nicest smile, professional as it was, and
patted my tweed shoulder with her long fingers, then
headed toward her corner with a stride that would make a
prelate pee his trousers.

The next night I was standing there with a cardboard
coffee warming one hand, and a leather-bound copy of
Maud in the other, when the same fellow stopped his car in
front of me. The passenger-side window lowered without a
sound, and he leaned over as best he could with his seatbelt
on.

"How much?" he asked.

Of course I had thought about this, and had even come
to a decision, but at that moment I could not remember
what decision I had come to.

"Negotiable," I said.

"So, negotiate," he said.

"Hundred dollars."

"Fifty."

"Okay." I had been standing on that corner for two
weeks without a sale.

"Get in."

I was as awkward as always, what with my briefcase, and
Maud and coffee. Over the past two weeks, and during my

71

research the week before that, I had seen tall young women on high spiky shoes slip into the passenger seats of sedans and jeeps and convertibles with a flourish of long naked legs and rippling hair. I banged my knee, dropped my coffee to the curb and took three tries at closing the door. I didnt even try to do the seatbelt.

"Are we going to your place or a dark parking-lot?" the guy asked.

"What? I mean what?" Things were still falling off my lap, etcetera.

"Usually we go to their place or a dark parking-lot," he said. "Some of them dont want anyone going to their place. I never go to my place."

"Oh, I never go to my place on a first date," I said.

Which didnt make a lot of sense, because if I was going to sell my mind for $50 the least I could do was let my reference books do half the work.

He pulled the car, and now I saw that it was a sports utility vehicle, into a lot down by the north side of False Creek.

"What sports do you find your vehicle useful for?"

"I dont know what you're talking about," he said, and he turned off the key. The lights went out and a glimmer was noticeable on the water. On the south side of False Creek young marrieds put their white plastic bags of fresh farm vegetables on the floor and began to consume three-dollar cups of coffee.

"I dont do any sports," said the guy. He was ducking his head under his retracting seatbelt.

"Well, you have a sports utility vehicle," I said.

"I dont know what you're talking about," he said. "This dont seem much like $50 worth of mind to me."

I seized the opportunity to appear on top of the moment.

"The transaction starts when you hand me $50," I said.

He was a little overweight, and probably short, and shifted and heaved in the bucket seat as he reached into a side pants pocket for his thick wallet. He gave me two twenties, a five, three loonies and some silver.

"That's what I've got," he said.

"I'll go 55 minutes," I said. I was wondering every second, what happens next, what do I do? I remembered certain experiences in the classroom.

"Okay, start," he said, and he might as well have looked at his wristwatch.

"You interested in the Austro-French Piedmontese war?" I asked, and a voice inside me asked why the hell I would come up with that.

He eyeballed me, then looked ahead at the shimmer in the black water. He shuffled his body behind the driver's wheel, and put the palm of his right hand on his right thigh. Was he getting ready to put in on my left thigh? What the hell is the protocol, I asked myself.

I shuffled my body in the passenger seat.

"Well, it seems that an Italian patriot named Felice Orsini tried to assassinate the Habsburg emperor Franz-Josef. People were always trying to assassinate the Habsburg emperor. But when Napoléon III of France found out about it, he remembered that in his youth he too had fought for Italian independence. The Napoléons were always crying for liberty and such, while pulling off coups d'état, and here was a chance for Louis-Napoléon to get in good with the senators he had recently dumped. So in a secret meeting at Plombières, in July of 1858, he pledged support for the Italian forces in the effort to free Lombardy and Venetia from the Austrian yoke. There are two villages called Plombières, in fact. There is Plombières-les-Bains, a dicky little place somewhat south of Nancy, and Plombières-les-Dijon, just west of Dijon. Anyway, the Italians also had England on their side, and could probably count on the Russians, who were pissed off with the Austrians for not being grateful enough for their help in an earlier scrap. Well, the Austrians blew this one. They should have just let well enough alone, but the emperor sent tough messages to Sardinia and Piedmont and ordered the Italians to forget it. This gave Napoléon III and Cavour all the excuse they needed to start the Austro-Piedmontese war. Well, both sides fought with stupidity and gallantry, and thousands of nicely dressed soldiers were killed, but eventually Napoléon beat Franz-Josef, and a little more of the Italian peninsula was removed from Austrian ownership. Then, of course the Austrians had to worry about war with Prussia concerning territory in Denmark."

"Fascinating but confusing," said my client, still looking at the shimmer. The fingers of his right hand were tapping on his right knee.

"Interested in how the rumours of liberty in the north of Italy seemed to threaten the hegemony of the Pope?"

"I would find it fascinating."

"The Pope's people in Paris were concerned that—"

"I would find it fascinating, but I have to bring up a question that is bothering me," said my client, with 40-some-odd minutes still on the clock.

The thought went through my mind that if I had had students more like him I might have still been in the classroom. Imagine: a student that brings up a question. Of course I smiled now, and shuffled in my seat so that I was nearly facing him.

"Bring up your question, Mr.—"

"We dont do names in this kind of situation," he said.

"Of course not," I said. "What is your question?"

Unconsciously, probably, he now had his hands on the steering-wheel. He did not, at first, look like the kind of man who spends a lot of time in reflective thought, but perhaps the species accommodates to the individual—a look of systematic consideration fitted itself to his very high forehead, and he spoke, still looking straight ahead through the windshield into patterns of exterior artificial light.

"You claim to be selling your mind," he said.

"Correct."

"You're a mind whore."

"If you have to put it in those terms."

He took a quick look at me and then looked back at his shimmer. Then back at me, briefly.

"It seems to me," he said, "that with this Napoléon war in Italy, you are reciting a chain of events, a chain of events with a kind of cause and effect process, implied cause and effect, wouldnt you say?"

"Well, teaching is more than—"

"Teaching?"

"I mean."

"Here's what I'm thinking," he said. "All that stuff about alliances and battles and emperors, you could store it in your brain. Store it in your brain, and then bring some out whenever you need it."

"Ah, but it entails more than that. There's analytical thought and—"

"Bring it out whenever you want," he said.

"Sometimes it's easier than other times," I said.

His fingers were tapping fast on his thigh, both hands, both thighs. I was beginning to remember the stories I had heard from Danielle about bad tricks. No, that was an exaggeration, I decided. My client was still looking straight

75

ahead, out the windshield, at the gleam. That did not make me comfortable, though.

"So what I'm saying is: that's brain, that's not mind."

"Tell us what you mean by the distinction," I suggested.

"Us? Us? This isnt a classroom, professor, this is a date," said my client. I was really wishing that I knew his name, so that I could say his name at the beginning of each sentence from now on.

"Me," I said.

His fingers calmed down. Now he was running the palms of his hands up and down the dark cloth on his thighs. I reached inside my sweater and retrieved a roll of coughdrops from my shirt pocket. I extended it toward him and he looked and shook his head. So I popped two into my mouth.

I looked surreptitiously at my watch. Half an hour.

"The distinction," he said at last. "The distinction is this. Your brain is a network of gooey meat inside your head, very physical. But you do a million calculations, memory storing, arithmetic, sexual fantasies, and so on, with your brain. And it's *your* brain. It's a personal thing, an individual thing, private. You follow me?"

I nodded, sort of forcing him to look over at me for a second.

"I got a brain. You got a brain. All God's children got brains. One each. Some better than others. When you die, that's it. That brain is toast."

"So to speak," I offered.

"Whereas the mind—that is a: not personal, and b: not physical."

He sounded a little smug. Maybe a little apprehensive regarding how well he was doing, but also a little smug. Professors are used to getting that combination from people who want to argue with them.

"Proceed," I said. I had heard about johns who pay prostitutes a lot of money just so they can have someone to talk to. But this was a little complicated, this date. I mean it was I who was supposed to be talking for money.

He proceeded.

"Well, the way I look at it, the mind is something that just—exists—out there, and we tap into it. With our brains, I guess."

"I think I see where you're going," I said.

"Each of us can tap into various minds."

"Uh huh?"

"You've heard about them. The seventeenth-century mind. The female mind. The Northern European mind. Etcetera etcetera."

"The Habsburg mind and the Piedmontese mind," I suggested.

"Ha ha. So what does it mean when you 'change your mind'? I guess it's like changing your address or changing your pants. You move out of one and into another. That's mind. So that's why you cant really say that you're selling your mind on the street, eh?"

"Well," I said in my defence, "I cant very well say I've got brain for sale, can I?"

"Climb the stairs, try my wares."

"What?" I didnt know what he was saying.

Now his fingers were tapping like crazy.

"I figure you ought to give me back half my money," he said.

"Why?"

"Well, I figure brain is worth a lot less than mind, it being just—a: physical, and b: personal."

"Ah," I countered, making the "ah" last as long as possible while I thought about my next move. "Ah, but mind, well, you can just tap into mind, like the Internet. But brain is individual. If you get someone to deliver brain, that's a service. The provider has to make a living, eh?"

He was looking at me now, instead of his old shimmer.

"Okay, I guess you're right," he said.

I smiled.

"How about a kiss?" he said.

What the hell. I gave him a kiss.

Religious Knowledge
Cynthia Flood

"Silly old virgin and martyr"—thus St. Cecilia is designated at St. Mildred's. Her Day, the twenty-second of November, in 1953 falls on a Sunday. A weak sun shines. As always early morning brings peace to Miss Flower, especially after the night's tumultuous quest. Before matins she readies herself, spiritually and as a teacher, for the week. As her own Bible study this term Miss Flower has chosen Corinthians I:13. *Charity suffereth long, and is kind*—she writes out this and other verses to stash in pockets, handbag, prayerbook.

After Lights Out in the dormitory on Sunday, the ritual of St. Cecilia's Dirty Night will unfold. "Just wait until Dirty Night!" For weeks Amanda and Helen have heard rumours and snickers and odd pleasurable sighs. "On Dirty Night, you'll see!" Amanda wants to discuss and speculate, but Helen is silent.

Charity envieth not, Miss Flower writes neatly.

That night in the dark dormitory, on her back, Amanda Ellis lies naked. She gets an early turn, being one of the youngest.

Sunday mornings are also for devotional reading, the adjective used liberally: Richardson's *Preface to Bible Study*, novels by Rose Macaulay, Elizabeth Goudge's *God So Loved the World*. At *Screwtape* Miss Flower titters anxiously. *The Lion, The Witch, and the Wardrobe* is more to her liking.

Late November, the dormitory unheated—but the torches *flashlights* held by other naked girls warm Amanda's thighs. Her smooth private skin feels light, embarrassment, pleasure, fear.

Charity vaunteth not itself, is not puffed up.

Someone holds Amanda open. Fingers go inside a place she did not know of. To expand the view, someone holds a pocket-mirror.

More daringly, Miss Flower attempts *Little Gidding* but is quite dismayed and lends it to Mr. Greene in hopes he may explain it to her and notice her blue eyes.

Next in the drama, Amanda must walk down the aisle between the beds crowded with naked watching girls. Her heart bangs. The spots where her breasts haven't yet appeared feel huge, while the small territory between her legs, to date used only for peeing and number two, has swollen into a giant three-spouted delta.

With *Murder in the Cathedral* Miss Flower does better; there is proper history, after all, under all that poetry.

Bulging globes of flesh are Amanda's tummy and bum. The dormitory is one absorbed stare, though not urgently breathless as when pretty Tessa and prettier Rose glide by the peering beds.

At the invitation of Miss Gregson, Science, Miss Flower even attends a local performance of *Murder*. She is upset, thrilled, puzzled. (Miss Pruitt, Literature and Composition, does not go, having read Eliot's work and found it *in very poor taste*.)

When it is Helen Hepworth's turn for centre stage, Amanda squeezes her hand. It's slick and cold. Dew gleams on her white forehead; *paleface*, Amanda teases her when they play Indians in the beechwood. Helen gasps as the torch-beams touch her eyes.

Miss Flower studies today's appointed *Lessons*, turning with relief from Ecclesiastes' gloom and Malachi's curses to Paul, who delivers for the Hebrews a paean to faith's powers. Then in prayer she rededicates herself as a teacher. The Third Form is to study a few of the Forty-Nine Articles. "Please ask questions," Miss Flower whispers earnestly, rehearsing her introduction.

Helen Hepworth has knotted the cord of her dressing-gown, and when the girls snatch at the tassels she slaps them.

Miss Flower lays Bible and prayerbook aside. In watery sunlight before the mirror she brushes her hair—thin, feathery. (Later in life Miss Flower thinks *A perm might help* and then, correctly, that her crimped head looks unnatural. Girls giggle.)

Savagely Helen kicks at the girls crowded round her.

Beholding herself in the glass, Miss Flower raises a frilled blouse on its hanger before her slight frame.

By the time the girls peel that first layer of fabric off Helen's body, she is biting and scratching as well as kicking.

City of mirrors. In Paul's writing days, that was Corinth. Burnished metal the mirrors were then and shimmered softly, not firing back these sharp reflections. Miss Flower lowers the frills and sees her white cotton chest. At the memory of how her hands touched that bosom while on quest last night, a blush rises. She raises a plain v-neck blouse and checks the mirror.

Under Helen's pyjamas are her knickers and vest. Her shoes, doubly and triply knotted, still hold her feet. Bigger

81

girls, more girls move in to control Helen and strip her.

Yes, this blouse is more modest. Quickly buttoning, Miss Flower refuses to recall where these fingers went last night.

When hands at last slip under fabric on to Helen's struggling flesh, she shrieks so loudly that one girl, startled, falls back against a bedstead to split her lip and crack a tooth.

Miss Flower hopes that after general confession she may approach the communion rail inoffensively. She garters her hated lisle stockings. O for nylons! On go her grey coat and skirt.

Helen shrieks again.

At matins Miss Flower receives the wafer and wine, at noon eats mutton and boiled kale and roly-poly pudding.

For an hour she supervises the Third Form while the girls write their weekly letter home. This is a new duty; she watches the girls, some smiling as their nibs race, others labouring. Miss Flower writes too. She uses a larger script and leaves wide margins, and thus fills out the blue Basildon Bond.

...yesterday at tea Kate Gregson showed her holiday snaps from Donegal and the Aran Isles. I told her of the old Druidic beliefs, there and here in England. Mr. Greene is in School just now; he had a good deal to say about Stonehenge.

This week we will be choosing the girls for the Lower School's Nativity Play. Miss Hodgson suggests that our Canadian girl, Amanda, be Narrator, in spite of her accent, or perhaps indeed because of it, since the Commonwealth now....

What else, to her widowed mother? The weather. *Love, Elizabeth* appears on the fourth sheet—and there's duty, done.

Helen shrieks madly piercingly unstoppably.
On this St. Cecilia's Day Amanda writes to her parents.

*Probably I'll be Narrator. Then I'd be "essential to every scene,"
Miss Murdock says. Wouldn't you be proud?!!*

*In RK we are learning Articles. What a funny word. The
Professor writes Articles, doesn't he? Articles of clothing, article
anything!!! Cheese or chocolates. These ones are* Of Both Kinds.
Of Free Will. Of the Unworthiness of Ministers. Of Baptism. Of the Civil Magistrates. *Funny!*

Miss Flower notes the complete absence of humility and
goes on to Amanda's friend, Helen. She sighs, reading. A
puzzle, this bright Helen who slouches about indifferent to
poor marks and athletic performance and all criticism. Her
prep is routinely *lost*. "She is not even a good liar!" Miss
Pruitt exclaims.

*Dear Mother and Father, Thank you for your letter. It came on
Thursday. The weather has been quite nice. It has not rained
much. Today was roast beef and potatoes and carrots and steamed
pudding. The Fifth Form is going to see* As You Like It. *Lucky!
We won all our matches this week. In Latin, we have begun the
fifth declension. It is hard. I hope you are well. Love from, Helen.*

Helen's ungainly hand ekes out these 73 words to a third
page. At home, once, Miss Flower found a drawerful of her
own school letters with their patterned paragraphs, carefully kept by her mother. This memory swells into a dark
angry wave—then too Miss Flower hated to go home—
which overwhelms the questions her brain is trying to raise
about Helen's letter.

Helen shrieks. Throughout the dormitory building, mistresses hear her cries.

Miss Flower collects the envelopes and the crisp aero-grammes for India, Malta, Burma. All are unsealed. The girls jostle out of the classroom, and she reads every word they have written. Elsewhere in the School other mistresses do likewise. Then the staff lick and seal, for no letters are withheld from the post. "We are guardians, not censors," says Miss Pringle, Headmistress. At Sunday tea in the Head's sitting-room all report on *anything untoward* in the letters. Classics, Geography and Games dominate these sessions; Miss Flower feels Religious Knowledge's low status. Bitterly, it is her fault. Strong Kate Gregson, Miss Lincoln in peacock blue and nylons—all would listen, if *they* were RK! She is shy; no, weak; no, *cowardly*. Hear Miss Pringle rap the table so the cups jump! "Look *between* the lines. Girls know many ways to hide meaning." The Assistant Head takes notes while her spaniels Fred and Nelly slobber at biscuits. Often no action ensues, for the Head trusts greatly in *Time the great healer*, but sometimes a trunk call is placed or a pupil summoned.

Helen shrieks. From chairs, from desks, from prayer, from lavatory seats, from beds, mistresses rise.

Not everything untoward is reported. Once in a girl's letter Miss Gregson reads, *Mummy, make lemon pudding and be careful not to burn it.* Metaphor bangs in her brain.

"Brilliant!" says Miss Flower. "I'd never have caught on."

Miss Gregson lights a candle, and lemon-juice writing under Waterman's Blue tells all. St. Mildred's many-cubicled lavatories embarrass this child; she cannot perform. She seeks out the few singleton water-closets, but mean girls follow her and stand by the door calling names. "She doesn't need any more publicity!" Miss Gregson exclaims, and proposes that she and Miss Flower shoo the taunters away. They do, and deduct conduct marks for loitering. "Problem solved, parents unalarmed!" Science boasts. "And Miss P. kept in the dark. *Time the great do-nothing!*"

Helen's shrieks continue as the mistresses rush along the corridors and rush in to shout amidst the naked shouting girls.

After Sunday supper, a solitary walk leads Miss Flower to evensong on the BBC, cocoa, curlers, book, bed, and no questing. Helen screams until Miss Barnes, Games, slaps a cold wet flannel across her face.

Miss Flower has not arrived yet. In her room with soft music playing, she is intent on the pages of *The Man Who Would Be King*.

Helen folds and falls.

When the uproar finally compels Miss Flower, the dormitory is all lit up. Matron is everywhere at once. Limp on the floor, Helen stares unseeing, as if she were someplace else. Miss Flower recoils. The child with the split lip weeps and smears her face with red. Girls scramble for nighties, plead with angry mistresses. Furious, Miss Lincoln has laddered a nylon. Miss Flower is revolted by the hot hysteria and thinks *With so many, I am not needed here.* She returns to *Man* and wireless.

Helen is carried off to the San by Classics and Geography.

On Monday the Third Form starts on Article X, *On Free Will*. Miss Flower tries not to be annoyed at Amanda's many questions.

Also on Monday, authority withdraws from the junior girls involved in Dirty Night their tuck-shop access and hot water bottles on cold nights. Older girls lose pocket-money and all town privileges. Prefects' badges are cut from their tunics.

An extra bed is set up in the Dirty Night dormitory, and the mistresses rotate supervision duty. Soberly the girls prepare for sleep. At Lights Out, silence is immediate. Girls who wake to visit the loo feel uneasy because the lump of Miss Maywood or the sprawl of Miss Pruitt looks alien, while in the narrow girl-bed the adult herself feels strange.

In the San, Helen curls up with her face to the wall.

Repeatedly Miss Hodgson visits. "What is wrong with you, Helen? For goodness' sake, child!"

Matron, run off her feet with influenza cases, has neither time nor inclination to cajole this sulky girl to eat.

When Amanda visits, Helen sips Lucozade. From Morning Break Amanda brings stale buns and to make her friend laugh tells about Canadian oddities like Orange Crush, maple syrup, chocolate milk. Helen smiles but says hardly anything. Amanda longs to talk about the puzzle of Article X but instead brings her Indian box, so Helen can smell the sweetgrass and stroke the bright quills.

Good tone in School will be most quickly restored if lessons and games proceed as usual, Miss Pringle claims. "To resume *normal routine*—that is our aim." Her directive is congruent with Miss Flower's hope not to think of Dirty Night. Earnestly she prepares lessons, trying to predict questions about the Articles. Routine. Her mother's response arrives.

...Mr. Greene's age? Remember, men dislike women to exhibit knowledge. As the most attractive of the younger mistresses you may easily distinguish yourself. Remember, you are getting on.

Is it wise to feature a foreign accent in a traditionally English, indeed sacred performance? Will it not distract?

You do not mention in what company Miss Gregson travelled. Tramping about primitive islands does not sound very....

It is just as well that her mother has not seen Kate Gregson's holiday snaps of a dozen youngish cyclists, women and men, wearing shorts and picnicking on headlands and beaches—Fanad Head, Inishmor, Annagry. They laugh. Their bicycles lie companionably nearby. None, Miss Flower feels sure, is married or even engaged to any of the others. One photo shows a caravan where wildly unkempt children cluster and grin at the friends.

"Gypsies. Travellers." Then Miss Gregson asks cheerfully, "Care to come along on our next jaunt, at Easter? Kerry this time, Dingle Bay, Lakes of Killarney. Wonderful cycling, I'm told, and ruined cathedrals galore! You'd be most welcome."

Miss Flower blushes, thanks, promises to think about it.

St. Clement's, St. Catherine's—the drear days come and go. Wintry rain whips at legs; still Miss Flower longs for sleek nylons. Helen lies almost speechless, but says when Amanda runs in breathless after hockey, "You smell of grass."

Amanda describes the smell of cedars and pines in Muskoka. Brittle as spider-legs, needles cover earth and pink granite. "You don't leave tracks. There's no sound, either."

"If we were there, we could run away into the forest," Helen yearns. "We could be Indians."

No—unimaginable, an English girl, even this one, in Muskoka! Instead Amanda leans close. "Helen, why were you so scared at Dirty Night? Please tell. I could help?"

Helen's freckles look like pepper on milk. Amanda does not ask again, knowing her friend will turn away.

"In Yorkshire there are fells," Helen says. "They go so far away they look like the ocean."

Helen grows thinner. At her substantial desk, Miss

Pringle drafts a letter:

Dear Canon and Mrs. Hepworth, Although Helen may not be writing home this week, there is no cause for alarm. Preparations for the Nativity Play have been perhaps rather too demanding. She is suffering I think from a little nervous strain and is resting in the Sanatorium. Matron is confident that soon our Helen will be her lively self once more, and we shall ensure that you hear from her then in her own hand....

Miss Pringle sets this draft aside with another, to the parents of a new girl who tried to hide a note in her letter home. Surely supervisory fingers would not...? But they did, they did; Miss Pringle smiles. Homesickness, she has written, is "always temporary." There is no cause for alarm. Soon their daughter will learn to laugh at her own feelings.

Next day the Head hands the homesick boarder over to Miss Hodgson for typing but retains Helen. *Time. Wait. See.*

Helen lies staring in bed. Matron says, "The look on that girl would sour milk."

Amanda sits by her friend and tells about Muskoka. In the bush that begins at the end of the lane and goes on forever, the hot July air is sweetly perfumed with raspberries.

Girls who cavorted naked on Dirty Night walk singly and clothed to the Assistant Head's doggy-smell office. The spaniels sniff their feet as they confess. Miss Hodgson, in the shorthand learned in her youth in glorious London, transcribes. "Speak up, Angela," she says. "Pamela, go on." Then Miss Hodgson summarizes all into one terrible tale and carries this to the San.

Three times she asks Helen to describe her experience of Dirty Night. Silence, three times.

Miss Hodgson reads aloud, to Helen's back. "In broad

terms, do you verify this?" The blanket moves. "I take that as confirmation." Miss Hodgson puts her papers away. "The Head says you have been here quite long enough, Helen. Tomorrow, Sunday, you will resume your place in School."

Helen lies curled up tight, her back to the door.

With a sigh Miss Hodgson sets her report on the Head's desk, and then she takes her dogs for a rainy walk. Passing the Gym, she hears the Nativity Play in rehearsal. First sounds Amanda's voice, "Then said *Mary* unto the *angel*." The Virgin whines, "How shall this be, seeing I know not a man?" Fred and Nelly bark madly. Miss Murdock says, "Again. Not so *loud*, Amanda!"

After rehearsal Amanda arrives at the San, ready to amuse Helen by telling her how to disguise herself with sweet blackberry juices. Perhaps then, Article X? But on seeing her friend's back, Amanda comes round the bed and kneels.

"Helen?" Only the top of Helen's head is visible. *Mousy* —why is it bad to have *mousy* hair? Helen's brown hair falls smooth as Muskoka stream-water. She is sucking her thumb.

Amanda lays her head on the pillow. "Tell me."

Murmuring, Helen pulls the covers over her head.

"*What*?" Amanda puts her ear where she thinks Helen's mouth is. Through the cloth her friend speaks half-a-dozen words.

At ordinary tea, Amanda holds these ordinary words in her head. On weekends white marge does not appear; the prefect divides sleek yellow fat equally into thirteen chunks. The dark tea steams Amanda's glasses. At prep, also ordinary, she forgets Helen's words while declining Latin nouns, but in the long stomach-aching pauses of not knowing what on earth to do with dreadful sums, Amanda writes down what Helen said. Each word is common. In combination they appall. She erases.

That night in the dormitory Amanda stares into her mirror, wondering how she can look so ordinary.

In letterwriting on the first Sunday in Advent, Miss Flower observes that Helen droops. Subdued—but so is the whole School, still. The girl's pen does move. And Helen is always pale.

Miss Flower reads Janet, Tessa, Helen, Rose, Amanda, Belinda.... Then frowning she riffles back to Helen's gangly script. *But* the Fifth saw *As You Like It* last spring; this term's *Merry Wives* hasn't opened. *But* the lacrosse team's "utterly wet," hasn't won for weeks. Today—apple tart. Rain, all week.

Examining every downstroke and linebreak of Helen's letter home, Miss Flower notes the address in Yorkshire. There's a knock; the Canadian girl is awkwardly at the door.

"Whatever do you mean, silly child, you can't say what Helen said?" To avert tears, she offers a pen. Amanda writes.

Reading, Miss Flower flares scarlet from scalp to nipples. She stammers. Waves of heat flow. She tucks the slip of paper deep in her prayerbook and for reassurance touches Amanda's shoulders. "Leave it with me," the mistress says fearfully.

Amanda hears only the words. Relief, relief—her insides loosen so she must run for the loo before she goes to Helen.

To her surprise, Helen takes no interest.

"But Miss Flower said she'd...."

"You'll see." Listless, Helen does not want to play in the beechwood, so Amanda tells about blueberries. On the hills sloping back from the lake, you must look down to notice

90

the low bushes with their blue load. The berries are sweet but not sweet. Crushed, the fruit's a paste of blue and green, red-flecked. "You can play it's pemmican," and Amanda explains.

Helen smiles faintly. "How far into those hills can you go?"

"You don't need to go far. The berries are near. My mother makes pancakes with them...." But Helen has no appetite.

At tea in the Head's sitting-room Miss Flower reports on Helen's letter, identical to last week's.

Miss Pringle: "Do you recall the earlier letter so exactly?" Her tone expresses grave doubt.

Miss Lincoln: "Such laziness!"

Miss Pruitt: "She simply makes no effort at all."

Miss Murdock: "Although Helen has little to do in our Nativity Play, even that little she does poorly."

Perhaps Miss Flower could go to the Assistant Head? But Miss Hodgson exclaims, "Why, *I* get Shakespeare's titles all mixed up! A little mistake?" and gives her dogs more biscuits. This response is manifestly so silly that Miss Flower almost groans.

"*Fifth* declension?" Miss Maywood's voice is tart. "Little liar! We shall be lucky to finish the third by Christmas."

"Nothing in haste," pronounces Miss Pringle. "Next Sunday, we shall see what we shall see."

Miss Gregson opens her mouth and closes it.

Of the other, what Amanda wrote, Miss Flower can't speak. Not before so many, though her weakness shames her. It must wait.

After tea, as Science and Religious Knowledge walk to their rooms, Miss Gregson mocks, "*We shall see!* An imperial *we*." A grudging laugh. "Temporal power. If there were lady knights in *Murder in the Cathedral*, Miss Pringle'd fit right in."

"I didn't really understand what that play was about, Kate."

"Free will, I think"—but just now Science is not interested in that. "Hasn't it occurred to Miss P that the parents will think it very odd, the same letter twice?"

More often than that, Miss Flower fears but does not say. Feeling for her room-key, she finds *I will not leave you comfortless; I will come to you.* Shame burns.

In her cosy arm-chair she opens *The World My Wilderness*, but in her ears sound the only lines that have stayed with her from *Murder*: "the torn girl trembling by the millstream," and "This is the sign of the Church always,/ The sign of blood."

Miss Flower gets up to look in her mirror. Outside her window drip the red rags of the beech trees. To wear such colours! She must see the Head. She imagines sunshine and herself in blue shorts, astride an Irish bicycle. She must tell what Amanda has told. Her legs are nice, she thinks. She may treat herself to nylon stockings, at Christmas. She must show that paper. Can she do it? Miss Flower longs to quest. To go to Ireland. Can she *choose* to absent herself? Shorts. Mrs. Flower never even rolls up her dress-sleeves (maroon, deep green, prune). At her side, Miss Flower has always celebrated Easter.

By mid-week she still has not seen the Head. Surely Helen's parents will write, wire? Someone will act. All will be well.

At table she notices a gap by Amanda's place. Others notice too. Helen, found and rebuked, says mutinously, "I'm not hungry." Because she has had *rather a rough go*, the matter is not pursued.

Amanda cannot imagine such a state. "I'll help you eat!"

Helen makes a face and shrugs, but when she does appear in Hall the friends giggle as they shove beef gristle around their plates and push rabbit bones under their cutlery. They sneak out bread and Marmite and apples, for playing Eskimos. "A cache," and Amanda explains about crossing trackless snow for days on end. As she listens to this tale, Helen's ennui falls away to Amanda's relief. Miss Flower hasn't said a word. This silence distresses her as much as Article X, but she can't say so to Helen.

Miss Flower hears from her mother:

...and soon you will be home. Of course I shall prepare, but I am not as energetic as formerly. I need you for so many things!

Lucinda J is to join me for a few days. With so few old friends now, I welcome her, yet guests are always a burden.

Prepare to be appalled at the Xmas decorations in the Parish Hall! Mrs. Heath has got the ear of the new man, and support from my committee has been lacking....

She sets this aside to reread a slip in her pocket. *Charity rejoiceth not in iniquity* is probably a Pauline reference to the notorious sexual corruption of Corinth. Questing would find a place in the city of mirrors, Miss Flower fears; Paul would be furious, revolted; but she cannot stop, to her shame.

Another slip reads *Charity rejoiceth in the truth*. Helen has gone to Matron. "She wants to *come back* to the San! Says she feels ill. Such lies! Such nonsense!"

On Saturday Miss Flower takes her turn in the Dirty Nights dormitory. She observes on Helen's dressing-table a photo of an unremarkable man and woman before a stone rectory. Beyond, the fells roll beautifully away.

She does not put in her curlers before the mirror. Instead Miss Flower kneels and prays for strength, with her feathery hair sticking up between her fingers. The girls, astonished at first, soon sleep. Miss Flower tries to read, but through *Descent of the Dove* the Hepworths stare at her. The mother's mouth turns down. Her stance sags. The Canon grins. Even now that man may be polishing his sermon, and tomorrow morning in public he will stand like Paul to speak in all authority.

On Sunday before breakfast Miss Flower goes to the Head to pour out pity and anger and accusation.

"You take this"—Miss Pringle drops the slip of paper on her desk—"seriously? You give credence to this document?"

"Helen writes gibberish, Miss Pringle, she is terrified, has lost a stone at least, shocking, this explains her behaviour—"

"*No*, Miss Flower."

"But...."

"You fail to understand. It is my task to lead this School *and* to protect it. Some little girls have played nasty games." The Head's finger-tips dismiss them. "But this, Miss Flower.... Ours is a Church of England school. Do you propose that I go before the Council of the Church Education Corporation, to whom I am answerable, to say"—Miss Pringle takes a breath—"that I believe a lying and undisciplined child who accuses her father, a clergyman, of an unmentionable perversion? Do you know the term *scandal*? And how it can destroy a School?"

As Miss Flower stumbles from the Head's study, Miss Hodgson tiptoes fatly after her, a packet of sweet biscuits in hand.

"No, thank you."

94

"Helen *was* frightened on Dirty Night, Miss Flower. All the girls agree. Her clothes...." In between mouthfuls of chocolate wafer, the Assistant Head tells about Helen's knotted dressing-gown and shoes, her knickers and vest, and describes how Helen struggled. "It was...as if she knew what to fear."

"Tell me, Miss Hodgson, tell me what we can do?"

The Assistant Head's crumb-dotted face shows surprise. *"Do?"* On this Sunday Miss Flower does not care that Our Lady was conceived immaculate nor that the staff glance oddly as they move past her toward the communion rail nor that her hair lies limp. In letterwriting, she can't set pen to paper. Instead she reads in *Britannica* of Kerry's ruined monasteries, of a standing stone circle with cromlech such as she has never seen. Do those chummy cyclists sleep under canvas irrespective of sex? She needs shorts, a knapsack, boots. Would she look right? Sometimes Miss Flower wants, even more than nylons, a girl's tunic or a nun's habit: a comely sameness stating surely who its wearer is.

Miss Flower glances at Amanda's letter; little know-it-all, still fussing about *Of Free Will*. Helen's is the same as before.

"Nothing to report," she says at tea. At that, does the Head relax just a little? Later, in the privacy of her room Religious Knowledge at last confides in Science.

Not for a moment does Kate Gregson doubt what a suffering child has told her friend; for this, Miss Flower is grateful. Science rages at the Canon and Miss Pringle. She deplores, commiserates, shakes her head...and then has nothing more to say.

"Kate, what shall we do?"

"Be kind to Helen, of course! Hearten her. Comfort her."

Miss Flower gasps. "But Kate, we could get in touch

with her mother. We could go to the Council ourselves." Her voice shakes. "If we chose to, we could do a lot of things."

Silence. Then Miss Gregson says, "Two more years at St. Mildred's—that's my target, Elizabeth. Not a word to Miss P, but I can hardly wait to be off!" This is in a jolly tone.

"Off?"

"Oh Australia, Canada, Africa—anywhere still a bit wild. I've no plan, really. Just *away*." She rises and smiles. "That's why I take these cheap cycling hols, to save my pennies. Only two more years!" Kate is at the door.

That evening, alone, Miss Flower holds her pen poised so long that the nib scrapes when at last she sets down *Dear* and a blot drops so she must take a fresh sheet as the words rush out.

Dear Canon and Mrs. Hepworth, Your Helen, who does so well in Religious Knowledge with me, has perhaps mentioned me to you? She thinks you might permit her to spend time at Christmas with my mother and me. I do hope you will agree. Other girls will also visit, so she'd have company. My elderly mother would welcome....

In this Miss Flower counts five lies, minimum. Quickly she takes a half-sheet—*Dear Mrs. Hepworth*, a line or two— and tucks it inside. Miss Flower addresses the envelope to Helen's mother, praying. Then she writes rapidly to her own mother. To stop second thoughts, in her mackintosh she walks down the School drive to the pillarbox. The envelopes fall in. *I've done it.*

Helen does not do any prep at all now. Miss Lincoln, supervising the Third Form, is sarcastic. "You *are* a pupil here at St. Mildred's School, are you not, Helen Hepworth? Or do you plan to live your life as an ignorant savage?"

Helen's smile makes Amanda uneasy. *Still* nothing from Miss Flower.

"I can help you! Except for arithmetic." Helen shrugs. While Amanda carefully draws a map, her friend looks on.

"Why not maps of *here*?" Helen asks. "Australia—what for?"

These ordinary words sound big. "Shall I colour Queensland turquoise or mauve?" Again Helen shrugs.

Miss Flower carries *He forgetteth not the cry of the humble* in her pocket and in her markbook *Thou hast destroyed the wicked.* These stones from her Advent reading support her in stormy water, but she cannot on schedule teach *Of the Unworthiness of Ministers* to the Third Form. Indeed, the sacraments' efficacy is not less because evil men administer them—but she can't do it. Sad Helen stops her tongue. Miss Flower prays the father won't find her note. She prays the mother will write. She prays her own lies to the Hepworths may find favour with God as charity.

Tuesday ...*extraordinary letter arrived a day late, which upset my week. What have these devious girls been up to? Women! I told you of attempts to discredit me, but you make no answer....*

Wednesday ...*trouble you seem determined to bring down upon yourself. You are getting on. You do not wish to end like Lucinda, keeping farmers' accounts and taking in mending?*

Thursday ...*bewildering agitation! Why is this girl your concern? No good can come of your attempts. Believe me, I know. I know. None ever does....*

Miss Flower imagines Helen at home, the young face bent over the breakfast table, the freckles, the thin young back. Miss Flower will prepare a boiled egg for Helen. She will offer salt, milk, buttered toast. In this fancy, Mrs. Flower does not appear.

Friday ...*whether you read my letters? An incredible invitation!
Is our home to be a refuge for schoolgirls with foul imaginations?
Elizabeth, remember your own father! You are, of course, in
charge. You are, of course, the earner....*

Miss Flower has no wish to remember her clergyman father.

On Saturday night after questing she dreams that Miss
Pringle (in tweeds) is at tea with Mrs. Flower (in wool).
Tray, lemon, teapot are as usual, but the two ladies lift off
their heads and place them laughing on each other's necks.
Miss Flower is a biscuit paralyzed in sugar on the plate. Her
distress awakens her. A second questing follows, rapturous,
exhausting.

On Sunday Miss Flower writes a brief blunt letter home.

On Sunday the dreaded Amanda approaches.

"Helen's not your concern any more," Miss Flower asserts,
a much-practiced line. "We have the matter in hand."

The child opens her mouth; Miss Flower's hand rises. *No.*
"Please, something else? *Free Will.*" Amanda is agitated. "If
we can't be good unless Christ *prevents* us, why doesn't He?"

"Be careful, Amanda! Sometimes we are so blind that
Christ cannot reach us. We see nothing."

"But Miss Flower, Article X says we can't be *un*wicked
unless He helps us!" Her eyes shine with corrupt enquiring
innocence.

"Heresy! You mustn't ask that!"

The child's eyes widen. Flustered, the mistress of Religious Knowledge tries to explain, but her words splutter
into such a garble of anger and confused theology that
Amanda goes away crying in bewilderment. Miss Flower
herself cries for very shame. To *bear, hope, believe, endure*—

clearly she can do none of these. She has failed in charity. She sees *through a glass, darkly.* She has not the most minimal capacity for virginity or martyrdom.

All the Third Form's letters go to the post unread.

"Nothing untoward," Miss Flower reports. Others note that Helen's presence at lessons, meals, even morning prayers is ever more erratic. Miss Pringle frowns. Miss Hodgson's pencil moves.

On Wednesday Miss Flower leaves her letters unread till evening. Before the mirror she sets her hair, then sips cocoa.

...traipsing about in Irish dirt! Christmas is to be spoiled—and you now propose to spend Easter with strangers? How can....

Her mother's many pages slip to the floor as Miss Flower opens another envelope. Helen's mother says *Yes.*

Clear joy flows through Miss Flower. Overwhelmed by happiness she slides to her knees and offers deep, grateful thanks for being allowed even a little, even for a week out of a young damaged life, to protect Helen. At Christmas the girl will eat her boiled eggs in Miss Flower's home. There at last a child will sleep safely and sing carols of joy. Seven days! And at Easter Helen might come bicycling in Ireland? Kate Gregson's good heart would be willing, Miss Flower is sure. Then next summer....

Footsteps snap down the passage to her door. *Rap!*

"Helen Hepworth has not been seen since breakfast," states the Head. "Twelve hours. She has hoarded food to take along."

Boiled eggs roll away, roll away.

"The Ellis child"—Miss Pringle pulls the ear of Amanda, red-eyed beside her—"has given her money. Do you hear? The girl has run off. Disappeared." The Head gestures

99

toward the night.

Nylons run away over green hills that dislimn in a moment, as do bell-towers and blue cotton shorts and a bicycle.

"The Canon says that this week Helen's letter was only blank paper. His wife was too distraught to speak to me. And *you* wrote to her? Miss Flower, who do you think you are?"

Mrs. Flower's hands tighten round her daughter's wrists so she can never never touch herself again.

"Further, Mrs. Ellis has telephoned. It seems Amanda's letter told a very strange tale." Out of the dark corridor the Head glares and other mistresses gather behind her. "You have failed to report, Miss Flower. What have you done?"

"She didn't do *anything*," sobs Amanda. "Nothing, nothing!"

The Alcoholist

Bill Gaston

Lyle van Luven typically got into these arguments with his
employers. And typically he kept a civil tongue, simply
explaining himself as he had so often before. Which over
the years hadn't gotten any easier—how to explain colour
to the blind?

"I am not a brewmaster," van Luven began, choosing *via
negativa*, "nor am I a chemist. Nor am I a slave to Bavarian
Purity Laws."

Again he raised the ostentatious silver mug, smelled the
naïveté of its contents, put it gently down. A pain gripped
his abdomen and he brought his hand to the desktop,
quickly but gracefully, for support. He was explaining himself to someone named Peter Philips, owner of Vancouver
Brews, another venture into the microbrewery industry.
This West Coast was, apparently, still flowering with new
aficionados of beer, those ready to dismiss the chemistry of
Molson's or Labatt's in favour of anything whose label read
"handcrafted in small batches."

Van Luven stood in Philips' new office, which smelled of
its peach-tinted paint, so he would not stay long. One wall
was a window onto the brew-operations below; another
afforded a moneyed view of the North Shore mountains.

Van Luven had been warned of heavy corporate backing here. He could see with his own eyes that beer was not Philips' primary love.

"Mr. Philips, if you want this wheat beer of yours, this blond, to be *the best in the city*—"

"Country."

"*Country*. Then you'll have to introduce a less conspicuous, more subtly engaging—"

"Okay. Good. What?"

Philips had no time for intimacy with his beer. He wanted it whizzing off the shelves.

"It must be subtle."

"Yes. Fine. What?"

Van Luven had no stomach for further debate on the difference between "mass appeal" and "quality," how they were very nearly mutually exclusive, and how a business approach refused to consider this. In his younger days he would have lectured. That time in Toronto he had pointed at the belching distillery and shouted at them all, *"This should be your church!"*

"That's not for me to say yet. We'll be involving the nuance of four, maybe five, partial flavours. So—I'll ask you again." Van Luven paused in punishment. "How is it— exactly—that you want your customers to *feel*?"

During the circuitous ferry trip to his Pender Island home, Van Luven reread favourite bits of the Buddhist tantric text he was studying, those passages on *prajna* and *alayavijnaya* which both calmed and energized him for the way they described the workings of his ordinary genius. He suspected the current beer project might be his last. While his death had no exact time-table, the growing fatigue and pain would soon demand a decision from him. The Vancouver test-batches would be ready in two weeks. He sensed the best route would be to tone down the apricot hints, which promoted a cheap kind of acidic *fun*, in favour of a more bodied, after-nose of smoky oak. This would be eccentric in a blond, but all save the most deadened drinker would gain from it a homey warmth and confidence. Actually, they would gain this whether they were aware of it or not. There was a suitable hops coming out of eastern Oregon.

After Vancouver Brews, van Luven had invitations to work with a distillery in Los Angeles (pollution there making his throat constrict at the notion), and with a vineyard in, of all places, France. *Estates de Petit Rhone* had asked that, if he came, he keep his visit a secret. While van Luven's reputation in Europe was solid enough, there remained that Old World embarrassment over employing a North-American taster. All of which piqued van Luven's vanity, of course, and he considered going. He suspected their problems lay in the relationship of rainfall and fertilizer. El Nino muddied age-old habits. They'd had a scientist in and now they knew, as van Luven always had, that this was beyond science. But the job was some months away, which may be too late.

The extreme low tide, coupled with the heat of the day, offered a waft of percolating mud-and-seaweed that smelled deeply vital. It felt nutritious just to inhale. Well, it was. In any case it was the perfect tide to bag kelp for his garden, and he would have done so were it not for, again, the matter of time. He stood on his narrow porch surveying his vegetables, and the equation arose unbidden: how much more food would he be needing? This question broke down into smaller equations: If I fertilized with kelp today, would I still be alive when the garden reaped the benefits?

How many more meals will I want to make of that chard? Why not trade half of that garlic for more of Oswald's carrots?

Since they'd resolved their fight last year, his elderly neighbour Oswald had been almost aggressively generous. The fight had centred around carrots. Van Luven had traded some green onions and romaine for a box of Oswald's carrots, one bite of which informed van Luven of at least two chemicals which would make him mentally ill for days. Oswald caught him burying the carrots on the beach. After assuaging the older man's feelings, a long discussion about organic gardening ensued—van Luven didn't bother going into much of his own history, or talent, except to say that he had finely honed senses—and Oswald was won over. For two years since he'd been eager for van Luven to try out his organic this and that, which van Luven did, having to bury only about half of it, mostly root crops, which continued to absorb the soil's residual nonsense.

Oswald was fine as far as neighbours went. They often stood and chatted at the spot between their two properties where a fence would have been. And van Luven loved—loved—old Oswald's cat, an unnamed stray tabby. The cat seemed to like van Luven too, and at his approach was given to a display of coy and ribald that looked almost like humour, something van Luven could not recall ever seeing in a cat.

Van Luven took his steaming dinner of new potatoes, chard, and parsley onto the deck, to eat standing up. He didn't like so spartan a plate, but he was out of the Saltspring lamb, the only meat he still enjoyed. For a decade, the salmon hereabouts had been losing their élan, giving him only their encroaching lethargy. Tomorrow he would phone and order a hind quarter. He would like another few meals of lamb. The innocence of their romp.

To his right, van Luven could feel the pampered growth of his garden; to his left, on the rock outcrop, the quieter swellings of moss and lichen, which sucked their life out of deadfall and, astoundingly, granite. The otter family should be cruising past within the hour. He admired their enactment of an ideal human family—two parents and three children—in the way the parents led and coaxed and herded, and the way the loopy pups splashed and played disappearing games in the kelp. They no doubt suffered crude neuroses and various otter-problems, but van Luven couldn't see them.

He turned to take in his empty plate, stopping to stare at his reflection in the glass door—was his skin yellower, or was that the sun?—then at the glass door itself, which needed cleaning with vinegar. He eyed the missing cedar shake above his head, its gap-toothed look of poverty. It was natural that of late he'd been stopping like this to stare at and chastise his house, and his land. Easiest was this assessment of place, comforts, life-scat. Easier than taking stock of his accrued *being*—which inevitably led to the house-of-mirrors taking stock of that which was taking stock.

The heavy look of the house was Shirley's doing: post and beam, thick cedar siding, a house to withstand earthquakes and two centuries of weather. They'd built it as their summer retreat, though van Luven, certain he could never again live in any city, secretly knew it would be his home. Shirley, his third wife, now third ex-wife, was a professor of engineering. Her world was one of physical equations. They had seemed a good match, for his world was also one of equations. But while hers could be explained, his could not.

His influences on the house, for instance, could be seen in the six Balinese wind chimes (the diamond sound of which cured some of his more rooted depressions) hanging at strategic windows, and the uniform white curtains with their lemon trim. The undoing of their marriage had less to do with his insistence on bare stone floors than on his inability to explain himself. "Allergies" worked for a time, but the word grew thin, and was in any case a lie. In the end, him saying that "the spirit of manufactured tile makes me minutely insane" simply *sounded* insane. Nor could he explain how he knew that his sensitivity to the world was growing.

But it had always been thus. It had been a surprise to learn he was different from other children. While other kids joshed while munching two and three hotdogs, his one bite gave him the dumb fear of the slaughterhouse, visceral knowledge of a mix of mushed parts congealing in a tube. Not to mention an instant salt headache. Tropical fruits awarded him exotic moods he otherwise wouldn't have known. Sugar was a harsh and wonderful drug.

One straw that broke Shirley's back was otherwise funny, and she had laughed without mockery. Nostalgic one day, trying to better remember details of his childhood, van Luven had made himself a peanut butter and jam sandwich, wrapped it in wax paper, put it in a paper bag, let it sit unrefrigerated for five hours, then took it out and smelled it—and became instantly eight.

By the time he met Shirley, van Luven hadn't yet developed the liver cancer, nor what they now said was a tumour in his brain, but he was well into his cirrhosis. In this he hadn't been forthright. He hadn't been able to explain to his first two wives his love of alcohol, and why he "couldn't just spit the wine out" at tastings, so why had he thought it would be any different with Shirley? He'd tried. Alcohol, he told her, is not just alcohol. The alcohol in one beer is not the alcohol in another. Alcohol was not framed by ingredients, it was made by them. What was the yeast eating as it died, expelling its vital poison? What was its environment, what was its *mood*? These were questions more spiritual than scientific. More, what was the relationship of the alcohol to the human body? This affair was *not* consummated on the tongue. No, the only bed of this romance was found deep, deep in the body.

Harder still to explain was that, just as the truth of Calvados—good God, it was *called* "spirit"—was discernible only in front of a rustic fire, at dusk, in something akin to a hunting lodge, so the truth in a German beer was available only to those who knew to chug the earthy froth down, exhaling noises of satisfied aggression as you clunked the thick mug on a table, which would be made of wood.

He couldn't explain, but his proximity to spirit spoke for itself. It had earned him his money and modest fame. Almost anyone could feel in themselves the difference between three drinks of draft beer and three drinks of scotch. But how many could feel—*feel*—the difference in a Pinot from one valley and a Pinot from the next? Or the difference between 1985 Laphroaig and its 1986 sister? How many would know it had been stored months in a decanter? That had been washed with detergent? Or if this ice cube was made from spring water? Not on the tongue, but in their being? How many people *became* the trace of detergent, or the spring water, or the patient corpse of peat in the scotch?

Addiction was an equation too. In truth, a marriage. And disease its necessary divorce.

Van Luven washed his plate and fork, and came back onto the deck to watch the otters. Hit with a sudden bad pain—the one that penetrated front to back and effectively bisected his body—he sank to the deck floor and put his knees up. He took several deep, rough breaths. Some of the pain he still could manage to feel as "interesting," but most now he could not. The small you could own; the large owned you. Knees up, keep the moans low and steady, releasing. He had his heroin coming, at great expense, promised from a friend of a friend of Shirley's. (He repeated to himself the funny phrase—"shipment of heroin"—which sounded like bad television.) He'd been assured that if taken through the nose it would be enough for weeks of pain. Or if taken all at once, to end things. He'd read De Quincy and others, and wondered how it would be, entering opium's palace. How long would he stay, before the millions of angelic candles extinguished themselves?

He had tried for a time to let his senses seek out a route of miraculous healing. He'd eaten certain vegetables and herbs, and even leaves and grasses, tasting and feeling in these the birth and fresh workings of new tissue—it was for the most part a raw, giddy affair, precipitous in its balance between the toxic and the vital, and one that felt nauseatingly like his own gestation. Nor did it work. The playground scamper of new cells did little but bounce off a densely scarred and tumoured liver that felt more mulish than stupid in its determination to die.

Hardest to explain—and doctors would be the first to laugh at this—was his certainty that his cirrhosis was caused not so much by alcohol but by imperfect intentions, and by ignorance. Insecticides. Additives. Actually, the real poison taken in during his life of alcohol was the greed, the *lack* of spirit, of those who made it. This he could taste.

108

This he had absorbed.

The pain lessened enough for him to doze. These days he was always tired, but he could sleep only when pain let him.

He awoke to the squeak and bang of Oswald's screendoor. He decided to stay down for a while, though he might miss the otters. This light rain on the face was pleasant, though he wished also for music. In recent years he'd been exploring music's visit to certain of his tissues. He didn't have a medical image of where sounds located themselves, but time and again certain tones gravitated to certain spots in his body, elbows and kidneys and ribs in particular, and he could hear the sounds in these new ears and feel them influence how he felt about the world.

But now not even his wind chimes could keep him awake.

Colours of sunset told him he'd slept an hour or two. He got to all fours, then stood. The pain had settled enough for him to walk the beach. The odd yellow in the sky—was it real, or was there bilirubin in the fluid of his eye? Was that possible?

Van Luven stepped carefully in his sandals; some rocks were slippery, others were armed with collars of barnacles on which he'd often cut his toes. Walking, he studied the shifting planes of light coming off sand, off rocks wet and dry, off seaweed in all its curves, colours changing even as he watched them. It was true you never saw the same place twice.

He paused at the lip of the tide, facing out, his sandalled toes half in the icy water. To his left, in a patch of clean sand, were a scatter of prints where his otters must have emerged, a rare event. He could see in the prints' pattern-lessness their nosing and dashing about. Curiosity, whimsy. He'd missed it. Maybe they'd left the water because he wasn't looming at them from his deck. He could see lines where their tails had briefly dragged; children's tails, adult's tails. Tales.

Vancouver Brews. Should he try to give Peter Philips the best blond beer in the country? Should he give him a good beer at all? Despite his wayward day, some part of him had been at work and had arrived at a deep, beet-like nuance, followed by layered aromas dissolving by turns—salmon-berry, honey, faint leathers—to the oak finish. It would look blond but hardly taste it. It would have blond's effer-vescence yet something weighty and generous; a beer to dispel many an off-mood. But why should Peter Philips have it?

As if beckoned, van Luven turned to see a full moon rising over the mainland mountains, and it startled him with meaning. It looked, it felt, like completion. Without much thought on the matter, but some surprise, he knew it would be tonight.

He had never had much fear of death. Death was simple, surely: if there was nothing, he would not know it. If there was something, it would probably be much like now, for there was no reason for it not to be.

Tonight. How? He had painkillers enough. If there was a way to keep from vomiting.... He literally could not stom-ach.... If there was a way to exit with senses open, unin-jured....

It was a medium-sized oyster, perfect, and for no reason other than that he picked it up, spied a suitable rock and dashed it down. A quarter shell broke off, enough for him to get a finger in. The flesh was sun-warmed. Not constricted by the bite of ice or of lemon, its taste was grandly oyster. He knew that his tasting so fully the creature's flesh was all the thanks it needed.

Spinning on his heel, carrying the empty shell, van Luven understood that life could end on a note of humour. The whimsy of an otter. He traced his steps back to the otter family's scamper-ground and knelt there, studying. He pitched forward momentarily, dropping his forehead to the sand. It seemed he'd passed out, for moments only, a new thing.

But there, an otter pup's perfect paw print. He admired it for a moment, its heart-warming symmetry. Then eased the shell-edge into the sand, pushing gently, scooping the entire print intact. He stood and held it to his face—a paw print in a shell. This he would send to Peter Philips. He would include instructions that it be added to the initial vat, and that it would linger in spirit in all brews to come. He would suggest a label depicting nothing but a closed oyster shell—which was none other than a sealed promise —and that there should be no words on the label. A man like Peter Philips might even do such a thing. And it might even work. The beer might actually taste good. There were stranger things than this.

Van Luven stared possessively at his paw print. He would add—one thing more. The edge of shell was as sharp as it needed to be and, an interesting pain, he cut himself deeply on the thumb pad. One drop, two, three, onto the paw-print sand, black dots spreading in.

Now van Luven jerked back in surprise at himself. Here was something he had not properly tasted. With caution, and respect, he lifted his thumb, bringing it to his tongue. In the instant of taste, he knew what he would do.

Softly licking his lips, he steadied his hunger. Taking

shallow breaths, he rose in courage, muscle. He took a deeper breath, held it, and under the rising full moon the shell sank deeply into his wrist.

He didn't have to suck, he had only to receive the rush, to swallow in suckling rhythm to his heart beat. His continuous stream. In its taste, the truth of a mirror. The hot bronze of all he'd known. Van Luven went easily to the sand, the river of himself leaving no room for any more effort, or thought.

the first motion of love

Kevin Armstrong

Mr. C.K. Stead
1011 Byrant Street
Christchurch, New Zealand

Dear Mr. Stead,

A symptom of too many books as a child is the belief you can live in one, where each journey has a beginning, an end, and resolutions as inevitable as the next chapter. I'd been in Fiji four weeks when I woke beside a rose-scented woman on someone else's yacht and realized my travels had evolved past some superfluous and sequential string of adventures into life. I left Canada fifteen months ago and there *are* stories plotting a path over long blue miles of ocean, but what this letter concerns is stories read rather than written, and those still to be written.

Mr. Stead, I had never heard of you before, but your collection *The Blind Blonde With Candles In Her Hair* impaled me with truth. In a few stories you articulated the most important elements of my life; in fact, you may have even saved my life. But I do not want to get ahead of myself, nor discuss my proposal until we have been properly introduced.

First, my presence in New Zealand. Fate brought Mary and me together in a heat-sink jazz club in Suva, Fiji's capital. She and her two Kiwi girlfriends were vacationing, and I escorted them back to the yacht I had recently been hired to tend. Despite her youthful appearance, Mary is much older than I; her every move bespeaks experience encapsulating a loving and generous core. Judging by the sheer number and variety of male guests brought aboard over the following week, her girlfriends shared this philosophy, but I was too smitten to worry. Indeed, their stay represents the most pleasurable and educational week of my life. The day I returned to find Mary, her friends, as well as the yacht's more fencible items gone was a hard one. However, her notes' claim that, had she stayed any longer, love would make leaving impossible affected me deeply. For the remaining week aboard I drained the few bottles left in the shattered bar, and wept with longing. Oh, her taut thighs and acerbic tongue! Both my heart and the yacht's carpeting bore scars from our torrid affair, and I near wept with joy when, on their return, my employers had me extradited to the country of my choice on grounds of solicitation and gross negligence. Rather than return east, I followed love west.

Your book jacket did not mention just where in New Zealand you are living now, but for an Albertan from the wide expanse of the prairies, N.Z. is a small place. Tell me, Mr. Stead, can a town with a few pleasant acres be considered picturesque? Yes, Keri Keri has that pretty little valley with the river, marina, and New Zealand's oldest stone building, but what else? One-level shopping plazas. An abridged main street. It was a point of pride for me that in the week spent with Mary, I never once set foot in the Old Stone Store. After all, I'm a traveller, not a tourist.

I should add that Mary was overwhelmed to see me. After gunning back a second scotch, she had me explain just how I used the yacht's cell-phone bill to track her down.

From Auckland, I'd taken the bus north, then hitched a ride from the Keri Keri station in an old troop carrier full of beefalo. On seeing the address I'd written down, the driver grinned toothily, and remained silent for the rest of the ride.

The afternoon sky was mottled with cloud as I laid my pack atop the barbed-wire security fence of Mersdan Estate. Inside, the rolling grounds were lined by rows of fruit trees, and moving between them were a half-dozen of the most beautiful women I'd yet seen in New Zealand. With wicker baskets slightly larger than their bonnets, each wore a sleeveless cotton dress, their long arms sun-browned and graceful as they stretched for the ripe fruit dangling above. When I asked where I might find Ms. Frussett they pointed toward the villa just visible through the trees. Their giggling chased me downhill. A flock of ducks winged the air overhead, splash-landing in the pond behind the long, low building. Only as I beat the knocker on the huge wood door did I realize that a similarly huge, moustached Maori stood just a few steps behind. He was dressed entirely in black and was utterly silent. After recovering from my surprise, I explained my errand. He disappeared into the villa for some minutes, then returned and bid me enter.

The villa was wide and airy and built from eucalyptus, lava rock and mortar. The foyer looked more like a hotel reception than a home; a striking blonde at the front desk stored my bag in the capacious coat-room. Farther inside, a bar bordered a fireplace sitting section, behind which stretched a long, kauri wood dining-table. The whole back wall of the villa was full-length windows overlooking an expansive patio where several couples sat lunching. The men were well groomed and older, the women various but stunning. On the grass beyond the patio, two more women lay tanning nude on lounge chairs. From one swinging door, a blonde in halter-top and stretch skirt emerged with a tray of canapés and other morsels. Her stiletto heels snapped like gunshots over the stone floor as the Maori led me through another heavy door.

Marianne Frussett is an attractive brunette in her late-forties with a languid, regal air. It was amazing; just her taking my hand made me feel my troubles were over. After fixing us drinks from her private bar, she bid me join her on the plush couch near the picture window. Past the pond, vine-lined hills leaned into the horizon. A long, angled mirror beside the window reflected the patio scene back to us, but I was too awed by Marianne to question its purpose. Everything about her spoke of class and fine breeding. With a few minor edits, I explained my situation. She nodded sympathetically. It seemed Mary did occasional massage for her at the spa, and she well understood the girl's rebellious and independent ways

Over our patio lunch of calamari and crisp *sauvignon blanc*, Marianne described her operation. The combined vineyard, orchard and spa was a favourite for rich and famous men from New Zealand and beyond. There was no place like it for aesthetic beauty and quality of service, something I might remind Mary of when I saw her. Then Marianne bid me farewell and good luck, and minutes later, I sat beside her still-silent assistant in a black Mercedes sedan speeding toward Keri Keri.

I shall never forget Mary's face when she opened the door. Her eyes widened into dinner plates, mouth so agape the hand-rolled cigarette stuck to her lip flipped down and burned her shining chin. She spit it out, cursing, but barefoot, could only stare as the butt burned into the Welcome mat between my dusted boots. As I ground ash under tread, Mary glanced over my shoulder and saw the Maori poised beside the big sedan. She yanked me inside, slammed the door, then raced dizzily around sliding bolts and drawing blinds. When she finally turned to me, her first words were not of love or even "hello," but a warning never to go near Marianne or the Maori again.

Mary's house is a small, rotting bungalow in an equally decrepit ghetto immured by natives. Perhaps disappointment was inevitable after the splendour of Mersdan Estate, but truthfully, I had expected more from the woman I loved. The carpets were drab, the walls clean but marred by the abrasions of time. With its candlelit corners, red walls and blackout curtains, the therapy-room was by far the nicest in the house, if not a little overdone. The table at its centre looked far wider and plusher than the models I'd lain on at other spas, but was no doubt functional.

Mary is concerned what neighbours think of her, so would not let me play the stereo too loud. She is also obsessed with cleanliness. I washed my whiskers carefully down the cracked enamel sink. I swept up my errant crumbs. I fixed a piece of tape to the underside of the toilet seat with the word "DOWN" written on it as a reminder. Once, I made the mistake of walking nude to the kitchen for a glass of milk. Mr. Stead, I have never lived with a lover before, but walking naked always struck me as an important freedom, a defining part of independence. She made no complaints when her clients did so.

The men who visited Mary were an intriguing mix of what New Zealand has to offer. From the big-boned, black haired Maoris to near transparent-skinned colonials, all her clients seemed uncomfortable, almost furtive while answering my queries. As they padded sock-footed down the hall, I was repeatedly struck how men concerned with muscular tension could remain so ignorant of hygiene. I did not learn much from these characters, and considered it no great loss when Mary forbade me to speak with them, or, finally, to be anywhere near the house while she worked.

Exploring Keri Keri took half an afternoon, and having spent the last of my savings on bus fare, I did not have the funds to venture further. Mary gave me the keys to her Honda, but my favourite place was on the porch outside in sunlight or dark, reading, listening, breathing silence.

I've always been drawn to strong, intelligent, verbal, not to say literary women, as some men are drawn to rock-climbing, or hang-gliding, or canoeing down rapids.
—*The Blind Blonde with Candles in Her Hair*, C.K. Stead, p. 16

As was I. Mary was a departure, a gorgeous soft anomaly in my regulated web of a life. There are times, as I'm sure you know, when one feels ready for something, waits poised on the brink of some great revelation about life, though we may not know exactly what that thing might be. There are also times when this revelation becomes embodied in the figure of another human being, a standing, breathing, sensual piece of creation. Amidst the sun and sand of our tropical paradise, I so admired her self-possessiveness and sense of freedom that I fell as much in love with Mary's approach as with the woman herself. I sought to embrace a new way, to open myself to love.

But there can be cruelty to closeness. What could be

worse than having the thing you travelled thousands of miles for, finally denied you when it is mere inches away? C.K, I will not ask you whether you have walked in my shoes; for the worldly, such experience is no doubt inevitable. There is no deeper solitude than being both intimate and completely misunderstood, is there, my friend? I was halfway through the ancient kauri forest of Waipu when a wave of sadness near overwhelmed me. Afloat in Fiji, love had been our language. A simple touch was enough to imply meaning in all its subtle fullness. On land, Mary seemed a different person, as if sharing hearts was different than sharing a home, as if, after everything, I had no real right to be there. Weaker men would have given in entirely to despair. Instead, I raced back to the car and sped home. So determined was I to fix what was wrong, to preserve the love dissolving inside me that I tripped over the large pair of boots blocking the front foyer.

What I found will haunt me to the end of my days. Dressed in a loosely tied bathrobe, Mary sat bonelessly before the television, rolled cigarette in one hand, glass of red wine in the other. The room was laced with pot smoke; another cigarette burned in the ashtray by her elbow. I was halfway to the couch when the reverberating chord of a fart seared the air. But I recall these details only in retrospect. My eyes were riveted by her wine, by the three fat ice cubes floating on its purpled surface. As I stood, frozen, the toilet's whoosh behind the bathroom door perfectly summarized my emotions. I turned and fled, not bothering to slam the door.

Now I know what you're thinking. But as a writer, you are acquainted with symbolism, and how in a writer's mind, one thing—even a small thing—can mean *everything*. Since the day I arrived, a list of Mary's foibles had been forming in my mind. Dope before sex. Music during sleep. Salmon on toast. Herpes. In the steamy embrace of new love, such idiosyncrasies are unimportant, charming even. But in the cooler climate of my arrival, I found myself making more and more allowances, in short, indulging her. To err is human, to forgive, divine, but my God, *ice in red wine?* The irony was that with no place to go or friends of my own, I was forced to appropriate hers. Speeding toward Mersdan Estate, the landscape that swept past the windows was foreign, surreal. I felt both exhilarated and destroyed, stoned with emotion. Perhaps this explains why, upon drawing up to the locked driveway gate, my foot hit the accelerator not the brake, and the car plowed right through.

By the time the Honda stopped outside the villa, I too was a wreck. The Maori showed me inside, ham-sized hand on the scruff of my shirt. When Marianne spread her arms to greet me, I burst into tears. Even after the fifth gin and tonic, I did not explain just what had happened: I *could* not. I feared she might not understand symbolic import, and find me ridiculous and fickle. All I said was that I had seen something, that it was over, finished. To my relief, Marianne took pity, and took me in. The Maori returned Mary's blunted but driveable car, and fetched my rucksack of meagre belongings. The spa employees listened attentively to my woeful tale. Amber, the resident redhead, seemed particularly concerned and sympathetic, even giving me a free massage.

But that night, as I lay alone in a poster-bed looking through my window, the true degree of my plight took hold. The moon threw a cold, silver sheen over the pond and grapevines, the dark fringing hills. Everything was foreign, even the sheets, and I began to shake like an infant, asphyxiated by the unfamiliar. Slipping from my room, I snuck along the hallway to Marianne's small library. Here I found comfort in the old places. John Donne, Oscar Wilde; I read Eliot's "The Love Song of J. Alfred Prufrock" aloud and wept through the fifth stanza. It was on that same shelf where I found you, C.K., standing with the others in their somber rows, title tattooed down your spine, your hand-scrawled dedication to "M" for her "warmth and hospitality." And from the first story, the first *sentence* I heard your thoughts like my own: honest, direct, delving for truth.

> *One wants to say that things are like other things—a sky like lead, or pewter, and the snow falling out of it like confetti, or the petals of white roses. But if you grew up, as I did, in a place where snow never falls, then perhaps you recognize more clearly its uniqueness. That kind of sky is like nothing but itself; and snow falls only like the falling of snow.*
> —The Blind Blonde with Candles in Her Hair, C.K. Stead. p. 146

You cannot know what a thing it was, to read this on that cruel April night. After fifteen months away, I saw again the shadows of the riverbank climb the opposite shore, the factory chimneys down-river cast white smoke into the icy blue over frozen water. And far in the distance, a single gas flare. I knew it was Edmonton before you told me. In a dark library in a near stranger's house 10,000 miles from my home you gave me back to myself, and this I will never forget.

Not until the next morning was I caught wriggling on the pin of your implicit questions. I read and reread your descriptions of Alberta, yet it was those observations about writing in Canada that continued to question and fascinate.

121

Strange how in all the Can Lit courses I have surveyed you are the closest to pin down the negative reinforcement of the Canuck identity. Perhaps that is the answer, the ironic realization that our "anti-identity" is so illusive that it can be articulated only by those outside of it. How perfect. No, how perfectly *Canadian*.

That same day I wrote my first short story: the tale of a young sailor who follows his heart to New Zealand only to find that his lover works in a brothel masquerading as a spa. In tribute to your inspiration, I even made you a character at the whorehouse! For a solid day I honed, pared, polished. Then I offered the manuscript up to the one person I could trust.

The next morning, Marianne was too busy to visit with me, in fact something serious must have been on her mind because she seemed withdrawn. Her one question regarded my intentions with the story. Naturally I said I wanted it published. She remained scarce the rest of that afternoon and night, but the Maori seemed suddenly ever present.

My last day at Mersdan began beautifully. Over a light breakfast with Amber, Marianne appeared and suggested an ocean-fishing trip with her assistant. I was about to agree when Amber explained my help was needed in the orchard, and implored Marianne to postpone the trip until that afternoon. Marianne yielded, and soon I was being escorted through the trees by the same six nymphs I'd stumbled across on my arrival. The morning was clear and warm with the climbing sun, but the women were unusually quiet as we strode through the orchard toward the broken and now chained security fence. I was about to ask what was wrong when Amber drew a cell-phone from her basket, spoke a few curt words into the mike, then re-hid the device. Seconds later, the bent grey nose of Mary's Honda crashed again into the gate, the chain snapping like string. Opening the passenger door, the women shoved me inside, and, tires squealing, Mary and I rocketed back through the twisted gate.

Certain people should not bother lying. They do not grasp how the most effective lie consists mainly of truth, and subtlety wins the day. As we sped down back road after back road, Mary's tale about Marianne's plan for me was so ridiculous that her true motivation became obvious. That she would go to such lengths to win me back was touching, but as we screeched to a halt out front of the Keri Keri bus terminal, I attained total clarity. In that *gestalt*, I saw I sought women like countries, desperate to belong. But to become a part of anything—place or person—you must first learn your own soul's landscape. Like writers do. Like you do.

I reflect on the person I was a year ago and scarcely recognize him. How blind he was, how full of conceit. C.K., the touch of your stories has shown me sensitivity and subtle skill. I want to meet you, to learn from you. Your words have brought me this far: Please, take me the rest of the way. I ask not only for myself, but also for a nation whose tragic lack you yourself have recognized.

You may quite rightly ask what I offer in return. As a father, you have raised and written the stories of your three children as well as any parent can. Well, C.K., I offer another sort of story; unsolicited, bedraggled, yet full of promise. My dedication to be a writer is total: I will follow your instructions to the letter. You have been writing stories a long time, my friend. When was the last time you helped write a *life?*

My second offer relates to those words you have already written about my country. Your description treads soft and beautiful, but there are things you don't know about snow. You don't know what it was like as a child to walk out after a sound, fret-less sleep to find your world draped with a blanket to build with. You may not have noticed how with the first snow of the year a wind's soft breath is invisible but for the angle of the flakes. And how the trees, the Alberta poplars violent with gold keep their fire, shake off the white like dogs drying themselves, their life's heat melting flakes as fast as they land. It took me 24 years to learn a tree's latent heat. And what about newness, how snow collects on the most dismal of scenes to erase its sins like a blessing, in one great Hail Mary of white?

In exchange for not setting foot in Keri Keri again, Mary gave me money to go. This last stroke of reverse psychology was as transparent as it was generous; nevertheless I took advantage. Already my course to you was plotted. Once the bus reached Auckland, I phoned Marianne for your address. Currently, I am at Lake Taupo, and will be in Christchurch early next week. Marianne has sent her Maori assistant down with my belongings. I look forward to meeting you, your sons and Debra, your loving wife. At the least I might provide an intriguing hour in an otherwise average Kiwi day. At the most you may discover how well some strangers know each other.

Yours faithfully,
Bryce Mallard

The Art of Medicine
Charlotte Gill

University housing found you shared accommodation. The photo in the file depicted a rambling Victorian. A narrow brick façade, minuscule windows. When you arrived a woman emerged on the front step holding a bowl of chocolate pudding. She was strong-looking, tall and thick-limbed. Dressed outrageously in tight, unflattering pants and a ruffled pirate shirt. You noted her bare feet, grey-brown on the bottoms as if she'd been walking around in the gutter. And up close, her faint moustache. She introduced herself as Colette. You didn't know whether to believe her or not because she looked like a man in drag.

She helped carry boxes up to your new room. You scratched your head in the middle of this off-white cubicle, wondered where to begin with the modest heap at your feet. Girl, said Colette from the doorway, is this all there is to you?

You took time to inspect the place you'd call home. The bathroom, you noticed, had blackened grout, a fringe of mould on the shower curtain where dirty water had puddled. One scummy bottle of shampoo sat on the edge of the tub, its contents yellow and viscous as egg yolks. A zone in the hallway reeked of old cat piss. Colette had not thought to make room for you in the fridge. Here and there, on the steps and shelves, half-drunk cups of coffee stood and grew fuzz. You'd barely unpacked and already you noticed Colette's fallen hair, long wavy filaments of it, that clung and travelled on your clothes. The next day you would buy a can of Comet, snap on rubber gloves and attack every surface until it gleamed. Until it smelled nothing like human detritus. Nothing at all but disinfectant.

You pushed Colette's door open against a pile of clothes on her floor. Her room, bigger and superior to yours with its view to the elm out front, was cluttered up with books, creeping house plants, exotic wall hangings and the like. You scanned the mess until your eyes found Colette nestled under a duvet, reading. Nice room, you said.

I'm a fixture, she replied. Can't you tell? A grad student. She said she'd been thinking about her thesis for five years.

Why not just *do it*? you wondered. What on earth was holding her back?

Colette nibbled from a bucket of chicken wings. A midden of greasy bones lay arranged on the upturned lid. You hadn't eaten a thing all day, and your gut constricted and turned. You announced that you were going out to get some air. Oh, she said, be careful.

Don't worry about me, you assured her. You were tougher than you looked.

She stood up on her bed anyway, to demonstrate how a woman should walk tall at night. She showed you how to hold a key in your fist. How to poke an eye out if you had to. The pocket-sized can of pepper spray she kept at her side, finger on the trigger. She told you where to buy one. Colette, you could tell, was the kind of person who obsessed about getting raped and robbed by strangers.

Classes began. You showed up for all the requisite surveys: "Anatomy," "Neurology and Behaviour." You would begin at the very top, your instructors informed you, with the human brain. Eventually you'd work down to the intricacies of the individual cell. The ways in which it transacted the business of life. The ways in which it was invaded and conquered. From "The Art of Medicine" you would learn to listen and empathize, to pick up on unspoken cues. You would absorb certain principles of compassion. From "Medical Ethics," a sense of fairness and jurisprudence. *How?* you wondered. One was born with these talents or not. How could they teach you all that?

You began at the top and worked your way down. You perched in the lofty seats of amphitheatres, at a distance from classmates. Professors spoke rapidly through microphones, their faces smears in the distance. They whipped transparencies around on overhead projectors. Their numbers and formulae streamed before your eyes. You transcribed everything they said in flurries of scribbling. But would you recognize them up close?

You huddled in your room, turning page after page, memorizing the chapters of expensive texts. The doorbell rang, shattered your thoughts. You heard footsteps and voices, cursed the rigours of Colette's social schedule.

She ushered her friends through the draughty hallway and paused on the other side of your door. You heard the word *intellectual* murmured as if it were an unfortunate ailment. You felt flattered, then offended. No-one had ever called you an intellectual. You were no genius, you'd admit, but at least you knew how to work. Harder than Colette, harder than anyone else if you had to. You stared at your open book. Pure toil, if you stayed faithful, would get you through anything.

Bursts of laughter, music. The clatter of plates below grew louder, louder. You stewed, glared at your four bare walls, the empty shelves and your twin bed with its crisp, tight sheets. You were furious with Colette. More angry than you should have been. More angry than you'd been with anyone in a long time.

You stomped down the stairs to the kitchen. Colette had cooked for everyone and the mess lay spread on every surface. Two girls with clogs and long skirts slapped dishes through soapless water. They stopped to look at you. You stepped over someone kneeling on the floor. Someone picking shreds of pot from the spaces between the tiles.

You passed into the haze-choked hallway, forgetting your purpose. Almost everywhere you looked, there were toe rings and maracas, dreadlocks and hemp-wear. You heard a jingling of little bells. These were like no people you'd met in your faculty, like no-one you'd met so far.

In the living-room a guy in a corduroy jacket hunched over a guitar, plucked its strings languidly. Dogs sat panting on the furniture. Humans sprawled over the floor. Colette's guests lolled and dozed together in a coagulated mass, chins resting on hips, heads on stomachs. You watched for a time until the whole room seemed to breathe. Colette presided from an old, broken chair, her leg thrown over its arm. You met her gaze, and she put on a sage look as if to show you that she understood more about you than you did yourself. Her lazy, arrogant smile invited you in. You shook it off and crept from the room.

Upstairs you ripped your coat off its hanger. By the time you descended the music had died. You guessed by the way people darted and bumped that something bad had happened. That something worse was about to transpire. You wandered to the living-room where a cluster of people hovered in a circle. A blond girl lay at their feet, curled and pillowless on the carpet. Her lips had gone puffy and blue.

The guitar player glanced up, returned to his fretboard. Everyone was high except you. Colette arrived at your side in a panic and seized your wrist. What should we do? she pleaded. Her helplessness did not surprise you.

You wrenched yourself free of Colette's grip. Someone would have to phone an ambulance, go with the girl to the emergency-room. That someone would not be you. All around, guests tried to sober, bumbled around for coats and shoes. The exodus created a breeze, and you let it take you. You fled with the rest, leaving the front door to flap open behind.

You wandered the sidewalks to the cinema, bought a ticket to the midnight show. Inside you found steamy warmth, the smell of burnt popcorn.

Someone bumped your spine in the lobby, a hand grazing yours. You gasped, unsettled by anonymous touch. You whirled to discover a man who looked familiar, but whom you couldn't quite place. Sorry, he said.

You laughed involuntarily, your heart thrumming.

Do you know anything about this film? he asked.

Not a clue, you said. You'd entered without even glancing at the marquee.

Neither had he. He was draped in a leather coat—too hip for middle age, too expensive for you. He postured casually, as if he knew you. You felt you might know him, but you didn't. You wondered if he'd picked you at random, followed you in off the street.

After the film this same man intercepted you again. It dawned on you that this was Dr. Green, the instructor of your Ethics class. He faced you for an awkward moment before sliding his gloves on. He knew a place, he said, where you could drink wine, listen to jazz. He asked you to call him Philip. He had no idea who you were.

The bar was on the top floor of a downtown hotel. You shot up in the elevator, found it dark and decadent, upholstered in velvet. Scotches and ports with prices through the roof. You let Philip buy you an innocent drink, then two. You'd travel up and down the bar menu, he said, together.

Perfectly harmless, you assured yourself. As if such voyages were normal.

You turned on some charm, what you thought might be wit. You smiled and laughed at everything he said. Booze turned your insides slippery, to liquid. You could get to like him, this professor, up close.

The waiter came around at last call.

I'm one of your students, you admitted, pushing dams in the candlewax so it wouldn't melt away

Oh, he replied, wiping fingers down his cheekbones. One of my grad students?

Meds, you admitted. First year.

Oh, he said again. That's really too bad.

You woke at sunrise to the whine of the vacuum downstairs. It was a sound and a time of day you couldn't associate with your roommate, so you staggered down in pyjamas to investigate. You felt queasy, hungover. You shielded your eyes from the daylight, from the sight of Colette in her underwear. She pushed the vacuum over and over a rogue strip of foil. She caught sight of you and shouted, *what the hell are you looking at?* When you jumped, it pleased her. She went back to her task with renewed invigoration. You stood there staring until you couldn't bear it any longer. You bent down and scraped up the foil with your fingernails.

Colette yanked the cord abruptly from the wall.

What happened to your friend? You wanted to sound casual.

Who?

The girl who turned blue.

She's not my friend, Colette snapped. I don't even know her name.

All day the house remained strangely, beautifully silent. Colette unplugged the phone, and someone arrived later to change the locks. So thoroughly quiet, you knew it would last. Good riddance, you thought. Colette's friends did nothing but pilfer the fridge, monopolize the phone and piss on the toilet seat.

Colette moped and muttered to herself. Your paths crossed often despite her chilly mood. At every turn you blocked each other in the doorways. She glared at you in her phony melodramatic way that seemed, underneath it all, to beg. You could tell this much about Colette: she was the kind of person who thrived on admissions of guilt and ceremonious apology. She'd like the whole world to apologize. The kind of person who, if you swam out to her rescue, would climb on your head and drown you.

For days after that Colette obsessed with altering the décor, rearranging the furniture. She usurped your chores, pestered you with her sweeping and mopping frenzies. You let her. As an experiment you let your end of the bargain slide. Hair in the tub. Crusty plates and cutlery piled high in the sink. Until Colette pounded on your door. When you answered she thrust a dirty pot at your belly. I'm not your mother, she said. For fuck's sake, take care of yourself.

No, you thought, accepting the thing from her hands.

She wasn't your mother. Not nearly as bad as that.

During lectures Dr. Philip Green never looked directly at you. His gaze steered around you; he always knew where you sat. But off campus, at the bar you came to think of as *your* place, you discovered him as a newfound continent of charisma and sincerity. He bragged about a teenage son. And, in a diplomatic, off-handed way, to a long-distance wife who taught Women's Studies at an American university. He never praised your beauty nor your academic brilliance. There were no vague inducements nor allusions to extra marks. But from the very start you felt shocked by his confidence, by his quickness to touch you—first your hand, then your shoulder, then the small of your back. He'd done this before, and you knew it.

It's a bad idea, Colette cautioned. A very bad idea.

You assured her you were in control.

Good for you, she said.

Colette had given up on her classes, as far as you could tell, and enrolled in an assertiveness training seminar. You'd heard of such things—quacky, ridiculous. Assertiveness wasn't Colette's problem anyway. Her real difficulty was as plain to you as starch on a shirt. She couldn't sit still or be alone for more than five minutes.

After the first session Colette regaled you with details. She walked over hot coals without suffering so much as a blister, and she took off her shoes to prove it. Colette spread her handouts over the floor, marvelled at the things she'd discovered. *Negativity is the killer!* they promised. *Think positivity!* It's simple, she said, touching at your sleeve. I've never done anything so right in my life.

Seven hundred dollars, you thought, it better be right.

The next afternoon, in preparation for her second workshop, Colette booked an appointment at an upscale hair salon. She returned with streaks and short layers and a new skin-tight suit in peacock blue. She spun for you, said you should look on the outside the way you want to feel on the inside.

Good for you, you said in return.

As soon as Colette left in the evening you dashed to Philip's. You waited in the shadows of his townhouse—your own idea, not his—until his neighbours disappeared. You pressed his bell, heard its deep gong inside. You felt buoyant, lighter than air.

Philip appeared at the door and opened his arms for you. He smelled peppery and warm, like booze, like relief, like no other man you'd kissed before. He peeled your coat back and hung it on a hook. He put his finger to his lips. Inside you heard the zaps and pings of a video game.

Philip led you past the living-room. The son hunched in front of the TV, bathed in its cathode light. You struggled for a glimpse. The furniture of Phillip's life, all the rooms and hallways—the passing seconds seemed to splinter into an inevitable past tense. You let Philip steer you upstairs, past what you guessed was his bedroom, outside to the narrow balcony. There he backed you up against the wall and away from the light of the house. His hands roamed you, made you dizzy. You closed your eyes. When you opened them again he was inside you. Somehow you'd slipped one leg out of your jeans and your underwear, and now they lay curled around your ankle. His body, with its accumulated expertise, worked you over in touches until all your pores tingled. Your body starved for this, you knew, but your rational mind, pressed between him and cold concrete, told otherwise. This was a thing to do once then never again. You gazed out to the city skyline, an infinity of obscure stars. Beyond the sliding glass a phone twittered. As Philip turned toward it his lips brushed your cheek.

After, the house was silent The son, disappeared. Philip uncorked a bottle of wine while you wandered around the living-room examining his hardcovers, his framed lithographs. Everything he owned appeared hard-edged, elegant and generic. If you had money you'd buy the same things. You wondered if that's why he liked you. Philip reappeared, caught your fingertips, tugged you down onto the sofa. He pressed his ear to yours, then snapped the two of you, together, with a Polaroid. Imprinting the flash, shimmering blobs on your retinas. There, he said. Now we're committed. He'd been drinking before your arrival. You were always drinking together.

You held the photo and waited for the positive to develop, to inform you of something. From the corner of your eye you saw Philip watching you in his drunken, sentimental way. The evening tipped in those seconds, slid down into a heaped mess. It was no surprise. Most outcomes ran contrary to the cleanliness of your hopes, your subtle engineering of moments. Your eyes locked with Philip's—you couldn't prevent it—and you understood something terrible and pathetic about love.

You stood up. Why are you running away? he demanded. But you could provide no answer. Everything between you seemed sad and compromised. You bustled to the hallway for your coat with its third button missing. He followed, pleaded with you to stay.

Outside the buses had stopped. You took a circuitous route home through well-lit neighbourhoods. You walked tall, as if you were invincible.

By the time you got home Colette had returned. With

company, a man from her seminar. She introduced him as Ricky. He wore a white shirt and a thin tie with khakis. Over this a leather jacket so worn it looked like melting chocolate. The muscles under his shirt were bulky, the kind men get from lifting weights in front of mirrors. He hooked a finger over his collar, tugged it down. You disliked him immediately for pretending to be something he wasn't. But why should you get protective about Colette? With her bubbly laughter and her shiny new shoes and her crossed legs.

Ricky smiled nervously at you, then at her. She introduced you as her *favourite person in the universe*. She said this to everyone, and still you were stupidly touched.

When you climbed the stairs for bed you heard them flirting. They sat opposite one another in the living-room, formal and legitimate in their overtones, as if they'd just come home from church. You envied them. The night had been strange. Your shutters blown open.

Nothing was wrong, and yet everything started to shift.

You began skipping Philip's class. He fired off an email in response. In his economical terms he claimed you were *damaging your prospects*. That you were, in practice, *cold and detached with peers*. He was wrong, you were certain, for exactly the opposite seemed true. Other instructors raced through proofs, omitting steps you hadn't learned but should have. The words you read slid through your mind without touching down. The boundary between your heart and your brain dissolved.

Ricky discovered Colette as an unstable isotope and dumped her in short order. Now you and Colette could be miserable together. She cancelled her registration for the *Power of Positive Thinking* and swanned about the house in

135

her long dressing-gowns. She indulged in half-day baths that drained the hot-water tank several times over. Her only guest was her acupuncturist. For him she lay prostrate, naked, on the living-room floor so he could poke her with needles. Through all of this she wept furiously. Colette and her great faith in tears.

When she sat buckled on the couch, surrounded by mounds of snotty, wadded-up tissue you wanted to slap her. *Pull yourself together*, you shouted. *He's just a man and an asshole at that.* Colette's face dripped tears. She twisted and shredded a Kleenex. She looked up at you with swimming, red-rimmed eyes and sobbed, *I'm pregnant.*

Oh shit, was all you could manage. What next? You stood over her and thought about it practically. What did she plan to do?

Just look at me. She spread her arms wide and pointed down at herself. What kind of a mother would I make?

You knew exactly the kind of mother she'd make.

A sickness crept into you, deployed its Trojan Horse. You lay pinned to the bed by strata of blankets. You imagined viral cells spreading out, locking on. They reinvented themselves with your chemistry, spelled themselves out with your alphabet. They multiplied. You pictured immune cells, white blobs in furious waves of defence and repair. Your troops signalled, sent bottled notes down rivers of blood to your brain. Taste nothing, they warned. Touch no-one.

Colette crept in and out, silhouetted in the light from the hall. She wiped your face with a cloth, forced you to drink hot beverages that tasted like nothing but steam. Then, when the fever drained away, she parked on the edge of your bed, crushing the springs, rolling you toward her.

She opened the blinds and pointed. Look, she said. Snow. It nearly glowed in the dark.

The next morning Colette emerged from her bedroom looking more sickly and bloated than ever before. She eased into an armchair, rolled a joint and got cranky. The smell of your soft-boiled eggs nauseated her. Sounds of traffic in the street nauseated her. The colour of your shirt made her stomach flip. She dispatched you to her herbalist with a long list of mysterious ingredients—lady's mantle, blue and black cohosh, malvacea.... Good lord, you thought, you'd be thrilled to escape for a time.

You drove across town to the Russian quarter and parked. Three stout women walked abreast, pushed you to the edge of the sidewalk. They wore heavy flesh-toned stockings, carried string baskets full of black bread. When they laughed their mouths glinted with gold crowns. The day was cold but dry. Something pulled at your gut: sadness, a receding thing, remnants of the flu. How long had it been since you've stepped out from your tight little routines?

The apothecary, a white-haired scarecrow, leaned in his darkened shop between a long counter and a wall of Mason jars. When you gave him the order he shot you a nasty look. You carried the paper bag of strange leaves and roots home as if it were something illegal.

At home Colette dumped the whole pouch into a stockpot, boiled it down to a dark, foul-smelling concoction that stank up the entire first floor. She seemed to know what she was doing. The stench lifted her spirits. You watched her strain a glassful, hold her nose and choke the liquid down. She slammed the cup down on the counter and groaned. Are you a witch or something? you asked. She said she'd had some training.

You tumbled into a familiar, anxious dream: you pawed like a dog at the foot of a dune, touched the hard edges of the thing you needed so desperately, the thing swallowed by cascading sand, the thing you could never quite see.

You woke up edgy, in a hurry to make things right. You showered and dressed, put on lipstick and perfume, and bustled to your Ethics exam in a big rush with your big umbrella that parted the tide of walkers. When you arrived at the hall, ten minutes early, Philip was nowhere in sight. You claimed a seat in the first row directly facing his lectern. The seats filled quickly, and you found yourself hemmed in by nervous, gung-ho classmates.

Philip floated down from the mezzanine. He set his briefcase on the lectern, clicked it open and spotted you. The test emerged, fluttered from his hand over desk-tops, then arrived in your hands. You smiled and winked but his eyes move flatly on. He floated off to talk to the proctors. You decided to focus on your blank booklet, the pencilled student jottings left behind on the desk. Someone told you to begin, and you were submerged in a sea of rustling paper. Your hand trembled from too much caffeine. You flipped your test over and read. *Identify ethical issues in the following scenarios while highlighting the potential legal implications of each....*

The first time Philip came near, you didn't look up. You smelled him just before glimpsing his trousers and shoes. He pressed a finger, one slim index finger, on the corner of your desk as he passed. He tapped it once and kept on walking. Your pen hovered at the top of your paper, but your mind froze. You could think of nothing to write in answer to his questions.

The second time he passed, you looked, let your eyes plead. Time was called. You heard sighs, chairs scraped away from desks. His left hand collected your booklet, your indiscreet scribblings. His right hand slipped a manila envelope on top of your arm. You tore into it. Found nothing more than a mid-term you'd never bothered to pick it up. You flew to the last page where his red pen had failed you. Where he'd written: *see me.*

You gripped the margins of this neat packet of paper, and it crumpled in your hands. You panted, so enraged you could barely see. The students around you cowered. They stood, fell away. Good, you thought. *Good.* You endured the minutes with Colette's air-headed mantras shouted out in your head. *Negativity is the killer*—its stupid uncanny pertinence kept you from imploding. Negativity *was* a killer. But you knew better in your moment of white-hot clarity that anything, good or bad, could devour you if you let it.

You felt anchored to your chair, made of lead. Dr. Philip Green leaned against the chalk rail. He glared at the clock on the wall behind you until the second-to-last student trickled out.

Why? you hissed.

He folded his arms. Because you don't know what you're doing.

It's not fair. Your eyes spat tears. You never warned me.

Trust me, he said. It's fair. He prepared to leave even as he spoke. He poked around for the armholes of jacket. He shuffled exams into his briefcase, and the sound of paper was killing you.

You wandered back to the house in a daze, found Colette dumping her potion down the kitchen sink. What are you doing? you mumbled.

She answered without turning around. Giving in to

139

biology.

Okay, you heard yourself reply.

Then she squinted at you through swollen eyelids. What's wrong? she wanted to know. She stepped toward you with her arms outstretched. You resisted. You were the kind of person who liked to resist, who took pride in resistance. But Colette locked you in her fleshy embrace. She didn't care about Dr. Philip Green. She didn't give a damn if you dropped out of med school. In the midst of these thoughts your eyes flooded. I failed my exam, you confessed. And you had no idea how to start over.

LEON ROOKE has written a number of works of fiction, including *Fat Woman*, *Shakespeare's Dog*—winner of the Governor General's Award—and most recently *The Fall of Gravity*. His latest collection of stories is *Painting the Dog: The Best Stories of Leon Rooke*.

ALICE MUNRO is one of Canada's best-known writers. Her most recent book of stories is *The Love of a Good Woman*. "Floating Bridge" will appear in the fall of 2001 in her forthcoming collection *Hateship, Friendship, Courtship, Loveship, Marriage*, and is reprinted by pemission of the William Morris Agency. Alice Munro lives with her husband in a small town in southern Ontario.

RAMONA DEARING currently lives in St. John's, Newfoundland, where she is a reporter for CBC Radio. Her stories have appeared in *Best Canadian Stories* and *Coming Attractions*, and her poetry in such periodicals as *The Fiddlehead* and *Malahat Review*.

GEORGE BOWERING has lately been writing amateur history and YA novels instead of short stories, though he has edited a number of fiction anthologies. His last book of stories was *The Rain Barrel*, and his most recent book is a literary memoir, *A Magpie Life*. He is currently engaged in another history project. Bowering lives in Vancouver.

CYNTHIA FLOOD has published two collections of short fiction, *The Animals in their Elements* and *My Father Took a Cake to France*. Her stories have been widely anthologized, and she has received a number of awards, including a National Magazine Award and the Journey Prize. Her first novel, *Making a Stone of the Heart*, will appear in 2002.

BILL GASTON has lived and worked in Winnipeg, Toronto, Vancouver and the Maritimes, and currently teaches at the University of Victoria. He has published four novels, three books of short fiction and a collection of poetry, produced several plays and won the CBC Literary Award. A fourth collection of stories, *Mount Appetite*, will appear in 2002.

KEVIN ARMSTRONG began writing as an undergraduate at Queen's University. He has worked on stories on scholarships at the Sage Hill Writing Experience and the Banff Centre for the Arts. A first collection, *Inside Passage*, will appear from Penguin Books in 2002. He lives in Vancouver.

CHARLOTTE GILL is a graduate of the MFA program in Creative Writing at the University of British Columbia. Her writing has been published in *Zygote* and *Event* and broadcast on CBC Radio. She lives in Vancouver where she is at work on a novel, *Broken Islands*.

DOUGLAS GLOVER is the author of four story collections and three novels, including the critically acclaimed *The Life and Times of Captain N*, as well as a collection of essays, *Notes Home from a Prodigal Son*. His stories have appeared in *Best American Short Stories*, *Best Canadian Stories* and *The New Oxford Book of Canadian Stories*, and criticism has appeared in the *Globe and Mail*, *Montreal Gazette*, *New York Times Book Review*, *Washington Post Book World* and *Los Angeles Times*. His most recent book is *16 Categories of Desire*.